ONE DOWN . . .

"You're a dead man, you bastard," Quint gasped through the pain.

"You didn't hear what I said?" Slocum hissed and brought the arm up again quickly, this time pulling it from the shoulder socket.

Quint gasped and cursed as Slocum held his full weight on the mangled arm. A second later Slocum twisted Quint's arm yet again, then released it so Quint was on his back with the arm splayed up behind his head at an impossible angle.

"Now, I'm gonna have my visit with these ladies, then I'll be on my way," Slocum said.

"You're a dead man," Quint gasped, rolling to his side.

"Get up and get out," Slocum answered.

DON'T MISS THESE
ALL-ACTION WESTERN SERIES
FROM THE BERKLEY PUBLISHING GROUP

THE GUNSMITH by J. R. Roberts
> Clint Adams was a legend among lawmen, outlaws, and ladies. They called him . . . the Gunsmith.

LONGARM by Tabor Evans
> The popular long-running series about U.S. Deputy Marshal Long—his life, his loves, his fight for justice.

SLOCUM by Jake Logan
> Today's longest-running action Western. John Slocum rides a deadly trail of hot blood and cold steel.

McMASTERS by Lee Morgan
> The blazing new series from the creators of *Longarm*. When McMasters shoots, he shoots to kill. To his enemies, he is the most dangerous man they have ever known.

JAKE LOGAN

SLOCUM IN PARADISE

JOVE BOOKS, NEW YORK

SLOCUM IN PARADISE

A Jove Book / published by arrangement with
the author

PRINTING HISTORY
Jove edition / April 1996

The Putnam Berkley World Wide Web site address is
http://www.berkley.com

ISBN: 0-515-11841-9

A JOVE BOOK®
Jove Books are published by The Berkley Publishing Group,
200 Madison Avenue, New York, New York 10016.
JOVE and the "J" design are trademarks
belonging to Jove Publications, Inc.

PRINTED IN THE UNITED STATES OF AMERICA

10 9 8 7 6 5 4 3 2 1

SLOCUM IN
PARADISE

1

The spotted pony seemed hesitant on the narrow trail. She paused to sniff the thin air every ten yards or so, judging it before resuming her pace. Slocum sat lightly in the saddle, not letting the mare's hesitancy get the better of him. They had traveled a far piece together and he knew her to be a good horse. Now if, after climbing the Sierras, she wanted to get a little skittish, he would allow her that much and maybe a little more.

They had been traveling for the better part of a month, slowly making their way higher into the mountains. In the last town, he'd heard of a place called Paradise and he liked the sound of it. Not a preacher's paradise you understand, where you arrived fresh from death, but a town where a fair number of people were making a fair living pulling gold from four identical streambeds.

The pony paused again, raising her head and flaring her

nostrils in the cool spring air. Wolves maybe, Slocum thought, then nudged her along with a touch of his heels.

By his estimate, he was a half day from the town. The tracks in the trail, cut by heavy wagons and large teams, were fresh and deep. And the center of the trail was well-packed, showing signs of frequent use.

A half mile along, the trail widened, nearly doubling in size. As he made his way along the widening trail, Slocum saw the sign. The sign itself was odd, because it was expertly rendered, like the sign one might see in a haberdasher's window of a large city. It was odd, too, because it was so chewed up by bullets that the single word of fancy script, Paradise, was barely discernable.

Wasting gunpowder and lead on a sign was a strange thing, to Slocum's way of thinking, but he'd seen it before. He knew it to be mostly the work of hands, blowing off steam after a few days of spending their pay on hard liquor and soft ladies. But what struck him as particularly odd was the fact that the sign was shot up from the back. Nearly every bullet had been fired into the back of the sign, as if someone or a bunch of someones had used it for a target as they rode out of town.

The trail cut to the left, then headed down in a gentle slope. Resting one hand on the handle of his Colt, Slocum let the horse make her way down. She no longer paused, as if she knew the scent of man meant a bed of fresh straw to stand in out of the forbidding night air and a heaping ration of oats to fill her belly.

Slocum's own thoughts were not so distant from that of the horse. He began making lists to himself, figuring on what he'd buy first: whiskey, bath, bed, meal, woman. He shuffled the things he wanted again and again in his thoughts, thinking over which would give him the most pleasure first to last.

By the time the town came into view, he knew he wanted his whiskey first and probably his woman last; everything else would fall into place when he had a better sense of the town.

It was one of the prettier towns he'd seen. What he'd expected was a half-dozen buildings with more canvas than wood. What he found, nestled into a pretty little clearing in the shadow of a mountain's stone wall, was a town that couldn't have surprised him more if he had turned that bend in the trail and discovered another San Francisco or Denver.

It looked more like a town that had been standing ten or even twenty years than one that had grown in the last six months. It was just one street, the single thoroughfare was lined on each side with two-story buildings, many of them with stores. And the stores had glass windows through which Slocum could glimpse the rituals of commerce taking place among well-stocked shelves and counters. In front of the buildings, put down as neatly as you please, were a set of new pine boards that were laid as straight and true as a surveyor's plumb could create.

Riding down the street, Slocum watched as maybe twenty people, men and women, went about their business.

At the far end of the street, beyond the livery and the sheriff's office, was the saloon. Slocum eased the pony to a stop in front of it and climbed down. He tied the horse to a hitch so new the bark had not completely been worn away and then stepped up to the boards and into the cool darkness of the saloon.

Inside was a long length of mahogany, behind which stretched a paneled mirror that reflected twenty or more bottles. A barkeep walked nearly the entirely length of the bar and offered Slocum a smile.

"What'll it be, friend?" the bartender, a sturdy man with a barrel chest and oddly skinny legs, asked.

"Whiskey," Slocum answered, leaning forward to let his elbows rest along the darkly stained wood.

"You care much what you pay, or don't it make a never-mind to you?" the barkeep asked, rubbing his thick-fingered hands across the front of the white apron.

"I don't much like being stolen from," Slocum answered, "if that's what you're asking."

"Steal?" the barkeep said in mock surprise. "Got the finest whiskey anywheres outside San Francisco, if you don't mind paying a dollar a glass."

Slocum could feel himself recoil slightly at the price.

"What's the poorer cousin to it?" he asked.

"Fine whiskey, too," the barkeep said. "Cost you four bits. And get you just as drunk, if that's what you came in for."

"I'll take that one, then," Slocum answered.

The barkeep nodded and offered a smile, then walked down the bar to fetch a glass and the bottle. Slocum took the time to study the bar more closely. There were four or five other drinkers in the place, miners from the looks of them. But they weren't what caught Slocum's eye. What held his attention was the fact that, if he hadn't known better, he would swear the saloon was not new. The wood-work behind the bar was finely aged and the mirrors clouded ever so slightly, a fine webbing of cracks showing through the silvered back. The walls were paneled with red paper that was faded from the smoke of decades.

"There you go, friend," the barkeep said, carefully placing the small glass of warm, amber liquid in front of Slocum. "That'll be four bits."

Slocum dug in the pockets of his canvas pants and pulled out the money, laying it carefully on the bar.

The barkeep took the money in hand and said, "You figure on having another, or you want some time to think about it?"

"Just keep the bottle handy," Slocum answered, raising the glass for his first warming sip.

The barkeep watched anxiously, waiting for an expression to appear on Slocum's face. When he caught a glimpse of a smile after the first sip, he said, "I didn't tell you wrong now, did I?"

"No, that's fine whiskey," Slocum answered, placing the half-emptied glass down on the bar. "How long this bar been here?"

The barkeep leaned back against the shelf and said, "Four, five months, that's when it was finished. Finished with the rest of the town, just about."

"With the rest of the town?"

"Yessir, built the whole town at once, Mac did," the barkeep said. "Brought in six hundred Chinamen, they built her. Did a good job of it, too. This saloon here, you probably want to know why it don't look new or nothing, am I right?"

"Crossed my mind," Slocum answered, raising his glass for another sip.

" 'Cause it ain't new," the barkeep answered. "Mac

bought her in Sacramento. Had her torn down careful like and brought up here in wagons. Insides anyways. Chinamen just put'er back together is all. Damn fine saloon, too.''

Slocum drained the glass and set it down with a nod to indicate for the barkeep to fill it again. ''Whole town like that, built by Chinamen?''

''Damn near,'' the barkeep said, as he refilled the glass. ''Don't worry though, they all left. Mac didn't build no town for Chinamen. Got two—no three—left, man and wife and his little China-girl, they own the laundry. Do a good job of it, too.''

''I was thinking 'bout doing a little gold prospecting,'' Slocum said. ''You know someplace I can get an outfit for a fair price?''

''Gotta see Mac about that, he can fix you up. Can't pay, that's fine, too, he'll give you credit. Go down to the general merchandise, see Mac.''

Slocum sipped at the second glass of whiskey. ''Mind telling me who Mac is, long as I got to see him to look for gold?''

''McDoblin, son,'' the barkeep said, now genuinely surprised. ''Where you been? Well, it don't matter where you been, you're in Paradise now, and you got to see Mac. He owns most everything in the town. Nobody prospects without his say-so.''

''I thought the claim was found by couple of brothers, Hale or Rale, something like that.''

''Name was Hale, but they're long gone,'' the barkeep answered. ''They put in the claim in Virginia City, but they never worked it. Mac, he bought 'em out. Paid a good price, too. That's what I heard.''

"So now this McDoblin fella runs things?"

"That's right," the barkeep said.

Suddenly, from the end of the bar, one of the miners said, "McDoblin, biggest damned sonofabitch. Wished I never heard the damned name."

Slocum turned to eyeball the man. He was big, and his wide-brimmed slouch hat and grizzled beard bespoke his profession as a miner.

"Now, I don't want to hear none of that talk," the barkeep said, a trace of panic rising in his voice. "Not in here, not now."

"You got a problem with this McDoblin?" Slocum asked.

The miner spoke without turning his gaze from the glass of whiskey in his hand in front of him. "I got a problem with him," he said, angrily. "But no more than any other man in town. I was a man when I came here, came to Paradise, I don't feel much like one no more. McDoblin."

"I ain't gonna warn you again," the barkeep said. "No more of that talk."

"You won't have to," A voice said from behind.

Slocum turned to see a well-dressed man step out from the shadows in the far corner. He was wearing a fine brown suit topped with a derby.

"Now, Mr. Crane, I told him," the barkeep said, genuinely afraid. "I warned him of that talk."

"I know you did, Dwight," the dapper man answered. "And I'll report it to Mac. I didn't hear any word, not one, of you encouraging him."

"What you planning on doing, huh? Killing me? Shooting me down like a damned dog?" the miner sneered, still not looking away from his drink.

"What I'm planning on doing is talking," Crane answered, his voice flowing out smooth and soothing.

"I ain't got no gun, I don't wear no gun," the miner said.

Slocum could feel his muscles stiffen. The miner now was as afraid as he'd ever seen a man, and was doing a poor job of hiding it.

The dapper Mr. Crane stepped between Slocum and the miner, offering Slocum a nod and a small, sad little smile. It was the kind of smile you'd give someone to explain the misadventures of a young child. "If you have a grievance with the arrangement, you know Mac would be happy to discuss it," Crane said, still speaking in a smooth, soothing voice.

But there was menace in the voice, too, and a menace in the way Crane stood so close to the miner. As he moved in even closer, Slocum caught a glimpse of a hand-tooled holster and the corner of an ivory-handled revolver.

"I ain't got no grievance, none at all," the miner said, trying to talk his way out of whatever Crane had to say. "Hell, I figure I'm just drunk, tired is all. Shouldn't be drinking at all, probably."

"You're name's Ragliff, isn't it?" Crane asked.

"That's it," the miner answered. He was still looking dead ahead of him, afraid to turn. When he reached for his whiskey, Slocum saw that his hand was shaking.

"And you've been working that claim of yours pretty hard, is that it?"

"I been working hard, Mr. Crane," Ragliff answered.

"Been bringing in my share, more than my share. That ain't no lie."

Crane leaned casually against the bar and produced from his breast pocket a small ledger with brown covers. He leafed through it slowly, wetting his finger as he turned each page. "I'd say you've been doing considerably less. Less than your share."

"Well, I ain't been feeling well, is all." the miner answered. "Not at all well. But I been working my claim."

Crane put the ledger back in his pocket and pulled off his hat to study the crown. "What do you say we just let this little incident pass?" he said.

"I'd surely appreciate it," Ragliff answered.

"And what say you just get on along back to your camp and get an early start tomorrow?"

"I'd say that sounds like a fine idea," the miner said hurriedly.

"After all, you're not going to find a cure here," Crane said good-naturedly. "Isn't that right, Dwight?"

"Oh, that's right, Mr. Crane," the barkeep said.

"Fine then, if we all agree," Crane said.

And a moment later, the miner was hurrying out the door, walking as fast as he could without breaking into a run.

The three of them watched him vanish through the bat-wings and into the glare of the afternoon sun. When he was completely gone, Crane turned slowly toward the bar and smiled at Slocum, "I'm Oliver Crane," he said. "I don't believe we've met."

2

It wasn't much of a howdy-do, but Slocum accepted it all the same. Despite the little drama that had just played out between Crane and the miner, Slocum extended his hand to Crane. He knew enough not to step into another man's business, but he also knew he'd remember what he'd seen. There had been real fear in the miner's eyes, and something had put it there.

"I was myself just heading over to see Mac," Crane said. "Be pleased to show you the way. That is, if you're done drinking."

Slocum replied by draining the glass in front of him and digging into his pocket to settle up with the barkeep. As he was drawing out his coin, something passed between Crane and the barkeep. "On the house," the barkeep said, showing Slocum two upraised palms.

"On the house, or on Mac?" Slocum asked back, hold-

11

ing the coin in his hand. Accepting anything from a stranger in a strange town could be bad business.

"All the same," the barkeep said. "This here place is his."

Slocum paid just the same and followed Crane out the door.

"We got ourselves a nice quiet little town here," Crane said as they stepped into sunlight. "Nothing ever happens here."

"Not without Mac's say-so," Slocum commented.

Two miners approached them on the boards. Crane smiled to them, touching a finger to the narrow brim of his low-crowned hat. "That's right," he said, in a flat voice, still smiling.

Slocum took in the comment and they continued along in silence. It was only a short walk down the boards and across an alley to the general merchandise. Crane paused at the door, letting Slocum enter first.

"Right in the back there," Crane said as they passed into the narrow aisle of the store, its shelves piled high with clothing and tools.

Slocum nodded and kept moving. It was clear now that Crane would stay at his back. As they passed the counter and the fat clerk, Slocum caught a glimpse of Crane in the mirror. He'd pushed the edge of his coat back, revealing the ivory handle of his side arm. His hand rested casually on the handle, which was stained yellow like old teeth.

Slocum approached the door and knocked.

From the other side, a booming voice answered, "Come in."

Slocum turned the wrought iron handle and pushed. The

door opened into an office. But it was like no other office Slocum had ever been in. The walls were richly paneled in dark wood. Along two of the walls were bookcases filled with calfskin bound law books. Another bookcase along a third wall was filled with green bound ledgers. The wood beneath Slocum's boots was shined to a high gloss, but covered mostly in a thick blood red carpet, and the desk was an immense slab of dark, polished mahogany.

The office looked like that of an Eastern banker. And, like the saloon, Slocum knew that it had been hauled up to the town and reassembled at great expense. But it was the man behind the desk who held Slocum's attention: a stout, barrel-chested man with a thick head of gray hair above his florid face. Staring out of that face, which was bordered by gray muttonchops, was a pair of small, gray-yellow eyes the color of pus.

"This here is Mr. Slocum," Crane said from behind as he shut the door gently.

"Yes, well, Mr. Slocum, it's a pleasure to meet you," Mac said, closing the ledger book which he was reading and rising from the thickly padded chair. "Name's Mc-Doblin, but every man in this town calls me Mac."

Slocum took the hand, which Mac extended over the desk. It was cold and limp.

"Has Mr. Crane here taken the time to introduce you to the laws of our fair hamlet?" Mac asked, sitting back down in his chair and indicating with a small flourish of his hand that Slocum should sit in the chair in front of the desk.

"I just sort of met him in the saloon," Crane answered from his position at the door.

"Well then," Mac said. "Let me take this opportunity

to officially welcome you to Paradise. And so saying, let me say that the laws in this town are the laws of civilized men. We don't tolerate the gross, the uncivilized, the unlawful. Not a bit.''

''Mr. Crane here, is he the law?'' Slocum asked.

''Mr. Crane is my personal assistant,'' Mac answered. ''General factotum, if you will. In your dealings with him, consider it as if you were dealing with me directly.''

Slocum nodded and waited for what he surely knew must be more of a speech.

''Do you obey the law, Mr. Slocum?'' Mac asked.

''I try,'' Slocum said in answer.

''And do you succeed? That is the real point, isn't it? Do you succeed?'' Mac asked, his voice low, his pus-colored eyes probing. ''To try and fail at something, that is like not trying at all, is it?''

Slocum met the two gray-yellow eyes dead-on and said, ''I try to be peaceful. Most times I get along with it fine.''

Mac paused, dropping his eyes to the desk and studying the papers and closed ledger book in front of him in thought. ''I built this town, Mr. Slocum. I built this town from the ground up. Every nail, every board, every pane of glass came up this mountain because of me. I brought them up through sheer force of will. I assembled them in my mind before the first wagon left San Francisco. I saw this town in my mind and I built it.''

''You've done a fine job,'' Slocum answered.

Crane snorted from his place at the door, but Mac silenced him with a glance.

''If I can build this town, Mr. Slocum,'' Mac said. ''Surely you can see your way clear to act like the civilized gentleman I take you to be. Now, what is your business in Paradise?''

Though Slocum could not see where it could be any of the man's business, he answered anyway. ''I was thinking of doing a bit of panning.''

''Hard work, that,'' Mac said. ''But I imagine you've done your share of hard work. You ever pan before?''

''A little,'' Slocum said.

''You looking to get rich, Mr. Slocum?'' Mac asked.

Slocum shrugged, knowing the chances of a big strike in these mountains was remote. At best, he was hoping for a small stake to keep him moving on.

''Surely, you want to be rich, Mr. Slocum,'' Mac said, his eyes lighting dimly as thoughts of money entered his head. ''To be rich and sit back in a fine restaurant in San Francisco or New York. A fine suit of clothes on your back and a dollar cigar in your hand. You'd like that, wouldn't you?''

''I wouldn't argue with it,'' Slocum said.

''I myself am very rich,'' Mac said as if he didn't hear Slocum. ''Do you know how I did it?''

''Saw it in your head?'' Slocum answered.

Mac stiffened for a moment, unsure how to take the comment, then continued. ''Exactly. I saw myself rich. And now I am rich. It was exactly that simple. I believe in dreamers, Mr. Slocum. I believe in dreams, particularly dreams of wealth.''

''Nothing wrong with that, if it all works out,'' Slocum said.

''It has,'' Mac said. ''I'll tell you my new dream. We will have an opera house in this town. And we will have one within one month's time.''

Slocum nodded.

Suspecting that Slocum was not interested in his plans for an opera house, Mac moved on. ''I will make you an offer, Mr. Slocum,'' he said. ''There's a spot up a little east from here on the creek,'' he said. ''As far as I know, it hasn't been played out. I own the claim. Anything you pull out of that creek, we split, seventy-five/twenty-five. How does that sound?''

''Who is the seventy-five?'' Slocum asked.

''Why you, of course, Mr. Slocum,'' Mac answered. ''I believe a man gets to keep most of what he earns by the sweat of his brow. I believe in fairness. Fairness is the cornerstone, nay, the foundation of civilization, of lawfulness.''

''That sounds just fine, then,'' Slocum said.

''And seeing as I think myself to be a good judge of moral character, I'll stake you to supplies. These, of course, will be paid out of whatever you pull from the creek.''

''That's plenty generous, but I have my own stake,'' Slocum said.

''Okay then,'' Mac said, and began sorting through papers. ''Let me give you this.''

Slocum watched as he found a clean sheet of paper and dipped the pen.

''This will give you credit in any store in town,'' Mac said, writing furiously, then signing the page with a flourish. ''That is, if your stake proves insufficient.''

Slocum accepted the proffered paper and carefully folded it to fit in his pocket. ''I appreciate it,'' he said.

''It's nothing,'' Mac said, rising and offering his hand.

"Mr. Crane here will point you to our hotel and the assay office. Tell Mr. Holmes at the assay you want the old Smith camp on my authority. He'll fix you up."

Slocum took the limp hand again and shook it.

A second later, he was out the door, Crane following him through the general merchandise. "You ain't gonna find a better deal anywhere," Crane said. "You're lucky he took a liking to you."

"And if he didn't?" Slocum asked.

"Nothing happens in twenty miles of Paradise that Mac don't have a hand in," Crane said. "You remember that. You take a notion in your head to start trouble, any trouble, you think of Mac first."

They were standing out in front of the general merchandise, the sun slanting west as if it were pausing before lowering itself over the treetops and mountains. "I'll do that," Slocum said, bristling slightly at what he saw clearly as a threat.

"Don't take it lightly," Crane answered. "If it don't help you any to think of that old man sitting behind a desk, then you think of what all that money buys him in a town he already owns."

Slocum turned to stare at Crane. "What is that exactly?" he asked.

Crane's eyes didn't waver for an instant. "It buys your life," he answered in a flat voice. "Mac, he's a fair man. I believe he gave you a good deal. Better than most. But you make trouble for him, you're as good as dead. You think about that. Ain't a man in this town wouldn't kill on his say-so. The hotel is across the way there."

"Appreciate it," Slocum said, stepping off the boards.

"Don't worry about your horse any," Crane said, still standing on the boards. "I'll send the boy around from the livery to take care of her."

"Appreciate that, too," Slocum answered over his shoulder as he walked across the street to the two-story hotel.

By the time he crossed the street and pushed through the hotel's doors, he had decided to put a bath and a woman off until the night. He'd been on the trail a long time and nothing seemed as appealing as the thought of a soft bed. Oddly, his talk with Mac had worn him out.

A thin man in shirtsleeves and a green visor appeared behind the desk as Slocum approached. "What can I fix you up with?" he asked.

"Room and a bath," Slocum answered.

"The bath ain't ready now, and we ain't got no rooms empty," the clerk said. "Maybe something at the livery."

"No rooms?" Slocum said. "You got two floors of rooms and someone in every one of them?"

"Got every room doubled," the clerk answered, holding up his hands in an attitude of genuine apology. "Can't even offer half a bed for a night. Like I said, maybe the livery can fix you up."

"Look, I got this here," Slocum said, pulling out the letter Mac had given him.

At the first sight of the rich, cream-colored paper, the clerk's entire attitude changed. He took the paper and read quickly, then said, "Maybe I got something. Cost you five dollars a night."

"Woman come with that room?" Slocum asked.

"No, sir, but I can get a bath for you in a half hour," the clerk chirped.

"I thought there wasn't no bath?"

"For an associate of Mac's . . ." he began, then ended with a wide smile.

Slocum reached into his pocket, pulled out a coin, and slapped it down on the counter.

"You'll be paying for this in cash money?" the clerk asked, shocked.

"Don't tell me you don't take money."

"More often than not, Mac's associates, well, they prefer to pay on credit."

"Well, I don't."

The clerk stared silently at the coin as if it were a snake about to strike.

"You gonna take that or no?" Slocum asked.

"I figure you don't give me no choice," the clerk said, still not making a move for the coin.

"Which room then?"

The clerk, glad to be occupied with something besides the money, pulled a room key from under the desk. "Room number two, first door up the stairs on the left. Best room in the house."

"Thank you," Slocum said, taking the key from the clerk's outstretched hand. "I got a saddlebag should be coming."

"I'll have the boy take it up as soon as it comes," the clerk chirped.

"Appreciate it," Slocum said, and walked up the stairs to the room.

As he put the key to the lock, Slocum wondered to himself just what kind of particular mess he'd gotten himself into this time. For a moment he thought about just walking back down and riding out. With any luck he could make Carson City in a week, maybe less. But that was a hard ride for a horse already trail weary, and when he made Carson City, he'd probably be walking.

3

The room wasn't much: a bed, washstand, and slop bucket. A cheap lamp with a cracked chimney was set out on a barrel that had once held nails. Curtains that seemed old, but were new, rose and fell gently in the breeze from an open window. It was like a thousand hotel rooms he'd been in before.

Odd, he thought, how all hotel rooms had a sameness, from the richest to the most modest.

Slocum went to the window, poked his head out, and took in a view of the alley. He closed the window and sat on the bed. He was just about to pull his boots off when there was a gentle knock at the door.

"Yes, who is it?" he called, as he pulled the first boot off.

"Got your bags sir," a boy's voice called back.

"Well, bring them in," Slocum answered and pulled the other boot off.

The boy opened the door timidly and stood there, as if afraid to enter the room. "Got them here, sir," he said.

"Well, put 'em down and close the door."

"Yes, sir."

The boy, not more than twelve or thirteen, and dressed in faded brown trousers and a worn white shirt, ventured a step into the room with Slocum's saddlebags. When he judged he had come far enough, he set them down slowly and made to leave.

"Ain't you forgettin' something, boy?" Slocum called.

"No, sir," the lad said warily as he turned back around.

Slocum reached into his pocket, pulled out a coin, and tossed it to the lad.

The coin sailed smoothly through the dimly lit room in a slow arc, then hit the lad on the chest and fell to the floor. The lad just stood stock-still, not even bothering to retrieve the coin from the floorboards.

"That's for you, boy," Slocum said. "For your bother."

"No bother, sir," the lad answered, still not bending to the money, not even venturing a look at it. The boy seemed to believe that if he didn't look at the coin, it would somehow go away, like an unwelcome visitor.

"Take it," Slocum said.

"Prefer not, sir," the youth said. "Mr. Mac, he don't believe in taking nothing extra."

"Well, I don't see Mr. Mac in this room, do you?"

The lad paled at the idea of going against Mac's wishes. "He pays me just fine, sir," the lad said, then raised his hand to brush a length of hair from out of his eyes.

"Mr. Mac pays for everything you need, is that it?" Slocum asked.

"Yes, sir," the boy answered enthusiastically, glad to put in a good word for his employer.

"But does he pay enough for everything you want?" Slocum asked.

"I don't want no more.than what I got or what Mr. Mac is offering, sir," the lad said.

"Nothing more?"

"No, sir," the youth said, now growing nervous at the turn the conversation was taking. "May I go now, sir?"

"Hell yes," Slocum said. "I ain't keeping you."

And with that, the lad hurried back out the door, afraid that Slocum might do him bodily harm or start throwing more coins or questions at him.

Slocum eased himself up off the bed and took the two steps needed to reach the coin, still unclaimed on the floor. As he bent to pick it up, he could hear the boy talking in a low voice and then he heard the voice of the clerk. Slocum couldn't make out the words, coming up as they did from the bottom of the stairs, until finally the clerk said, "Good boy, now you go back and tell Mac. Tell him everything."

Slocum unbuckled his gun belt and pulled the .44 from its holster. Then he stretched himself out on the bed, on top of the blanket, making certain the pistol was handy.

He did not remember drifting off to sleep, but he must surely have been asleep, because he was awakened by the sound of voices just outside his door. He let his hand slowly snake down to his side until the familiar grip of the .44 filled his palm.

There were two or them, perhaps three, talking drunkenly outside in the hall. The voices rose steadily as what was obviously an argument picked up steam. Slocum waited for them to move on or for the clerk to move them on, but they persisted in standing just outside his door.

Finally, he could stand it no longer. He did not make it a habit of involving himself in others' arguments, but now he saw no choice. Rising sleepily from bed, he stepped to the door. Now he was certain that there were three of them.

Slocum opened the door slowly, hoping that this alone would uproot them from their posts, but it did not. When the door was opened wide enough, he saw that two of the men, with broad faces, thick lips, and dark hair, resembled each other enough that they could have very well been brothers. The third was a timid-looking sort with a chin like an underslung bootheel and slightly bulging eyes. The two big men had the little one backed up nearly against Slocum's door.

"You gents mind doing whatever you're doing someplace else?" Slocum asked.

"This ain't no concern of yours, you sonofabitch," one of the mean ones said.

"He got a gun," the other mean-looking one said.

"I don't want no trouble," Slocum said, raising the barrel of the gun slightly.

"Well, you got some," the first mean-looking one said. "You got yourself a world of trouble.

The gun's barrel was just beyond the jamb when a thick, beefy hand caught it and twisted it back.

There was a fourth member of the party. And all at once, Slocum saw he'd been ambushed. The chinless man took off, hurrying back down the stairs.

Slocum pulled his finger from the trigger before it was broken off, and the man just in front of him moved in fast with his fists. Slocum dodged the first blow, countering with a rapid strike outward that caught the attacker square on the jaw and knocked him back a step. The other two moved in then, one with Slocum's gun tucked into his front pocket.

Slocum snaked his right out, catching the one on the left just above the eye, then punched again and jabbed the second hard in his ample gut.

Slocum punched out again and again, but the three of them just kept coming. They were so close now that it was hard to get a good punch out. With every step back he took, they matched it, staying close as the fight progressed further into the small room.

"Just git the sonbitch down," the third said, and Slocum felt himself toppling back under a fury of fists and kicks.

He hit the floor hard with two of the men falling on top. The third hung back, barking orders. Slocum fought as best he could, but these men were experienced brawlers and there wasn't much room to punch.

"You got 'im now," the third said, moving in quickly.

Slocum glimpsed something in the third man's hand, a length of board or an ax handle, and then the man swung and room exploded in a burst of pain and stars.

"Those boys did a helluva job on you," the clerk said.

Slocum left something wet and moved a hand up to his face.

"Damn shame," the clerk continued. "Don't try moving, just lay still.

"Bastards," Slocum muttered and tried to rise, but the clerk pushed him back down into the bed.

"Don't move, Doc said so," the clerk said. "Doc said for you to keep still for twenty-four hours."

"Where are those bastards?" Slocum asked, resisting the clerk's bony hand that was pushing him back to the bed.

"Gone," the clerk answered, pushing him down hard with two hands.

Slocum ventured to open his eyes and saw the clerk with a damp cloth in one hand and spectacles low on his nose in the lamp-lit room. "Gone," Slocum muttered as a world of pain exploded behind his eyes.

"They rode out like the devil hisself was chasing them," the clerk said, then dropped the damp cloth back into the bowl of water. Sheriff's gonna want to talk to you; Mac, too. We ain't used to such goings on in this town. Not at all."

"Nobody would have noticed what direction they were riding, would they?" Slocum asked, already knowing better than to ask the clerk anything.

"Now, let that be till tomorrow," the clerk said. "The doctor said you should—"

Suddenly, a thought hit Slocum. His hand reached down to his pocket and felt that it was empty. "Damn!" he exclaimed, sitting bolt upright. "Damn, damn!"

"Now, cursing won't help a thing," the clerk said. "Mac always says, 'Cursings the truest sign of a weak mind.' "

Slocum forced himself away from the clerk's bony hands and saw his saddlebag resting at the foot of the bed. The pain going off like a long shotgun blast in his head, he reached for it. Instantly, he knew it was empty. Swinging his legs off the bed he saw the saddlebag's contents of extra shells, eating things, a couple of dried pieces of beef, and clothes, scattered across the floor. The small Arbuckle tin of coffee that also held his money was gone.

"Sonsofbitches," Slocum said, already knowing it was hopeless. The men, whoever they were, were long gone.

"Now, you have to rest," the clerk said. "The doctor left strict instructions."

Slocum allowed himself to be pushed back down into the bed. "Damn," he whispered to nobody in particular as his head eased back on the pillow. The pain seemed to subside a bit, but now he felt the new pain of being penniless in this strange town called Paradise.

"The doctor left some pills," the clerk said. "I reckon now's as good a time as any to take them."

Slocum watched the clerk shake a couple of pills from a small glass jar. "What are they supposed to do?" he asked.

"These here are for the pain," the clerk answered and handed Slocum the two small yellow pills.

"Looks like he bought them off the back end of a patent medicine wagon," Slocum said, examining the medicine.

"Doc, he knows what he's doing," the clerk said. "You take them."

Slocum put them in his mouth as the clerk poured a glass of water from the pitcher on the stand. "They took all my money," Slocum said, after he accepted the cup of water.

"Don't worry 'bout that now," the clerk answered, rising from the bed. "Don't worry 'bout that now. Doc said if you move 'round too much, you're liable to loose up some blood clot in your brain or something. Blood clot kill you quicker than a bullet. I didn't know that.''

"That ain't true,'' Slocum answered, then felt the top of his head where a huge bump was rising proudly under his hair.

"It ain't?'' the clerk answered, anxious to gain whatever free medical advice might be forthcoming from his quest.

"It ain't true,'' Slocum repeated. '' 'Cause if it was true, you'd see every dry-gulching sonofabitch shooting blood clots and not bullets.''

"Mr. Slocum, I'm glad you got some good humor left,'' the clerk said as he turned down the lamp and headed for the door. ''Mac heard all about what happened, said he'd be stopping by in the morning. Seems he took a real liking to you. Mr. Crane, too.''

And with that, the clerk vanished out the door.

Slocum lay in bed thinking about what to do next. After a short while, he could feel the pills taking hold. A warm heat began to run through his body and the four walls seemed to pulse slightly. Then he became tired. It seemed that with each breath he took, the bed grew more and more comfortable. The thin mattress and threadbare blanket were like nothing so much as the thickest down bed in the best San Francisco or Dallas hotel.

Slocum could feel his eyes growing heavier and heavier and he thought, the clerk didn't lock the door. But then, he couldn't lift himself from the bed. The door, which was maybe two steps from the bed, seemed a world away. He would be better off trying to walk to Carson City.

And then he drifted off to sleep.

4

Slocum awoke fully dressed on the narrow bed. He lay there for a long time, letting the pieces of what had transpired come together in his head. As each fact of the past day fell into place, he felt his spirits sink. It was as if he were slowly remembering a dream that had somehow followed him from the land of the sleeping to the waking day.

Slocum allowed himself to open his eyes. A dim light flooded the room. By his best guess, he could say that he had slept soundly through the night. Certainly he'd slept long enough so that the pain from the blow he'd received to his head had vanished almost entirely into a dull throb. Mouth dry and limbs stiff, he raised himself, then swung his feet and legs over the side of the bed.

His boots were where he remembered removing them. He pulled on one, then the other. The sight of his gun belt, the holster empty, sent a shock of panic through him.

Searching the covers, he found no trace of the weapon. Neither was it on the floor or under the bed. He did not need to search the entire small room to know it was missing. More likely than not, it had been taken, along with his money, by the thieves.

Making his way downstairs, he was greeted by the clerk with a small, hopeful smile. "Feeling better, sir?" the clerk asked, stepping out from behind the small desk at one end of the room.

"Better," Slocum muttered, cotton-mouthed. "What time is it?"

"Four o'clock, sir," the clerk answered, then pointed to a large regulator behind his desk to back up the claim.

"Four in the morning or at night?"

"Four in the evening, sir."

"You mean to tell me I slept a whole day? What was in those pills, anyway?"

"Two days, sir," the clerk said. "You checked in day before yesterday. About them pills, you're gonna have to ask the doc about them."

"Two days, you say?"

"Yes, sir. The doc said to let you sleep. I wasn't gonna argue any, you understand, him being a man of medicine, educated in it and all."

"Two days," Slocum repeated dumbfounded.

"Yes, sir," the clerk said. "And Mac wants to see you. Said to send you around soon as you got up and about. He's been right concerned about you, and all. Seems he took a liking to you."

"I'll see him soon as I get some food in my belly," Slocum said.

"You can do both together," the clerk offered, "he's over at the saloon now having his supper."

"That's convenient," Slocum said. "Hell, that is convenient."

"Yes, sir," the clerk answered, his voice flat. "The saloon, it's just across the way there."

Slocum found Mac where the clerk said he would be. The old man was sitting in the back of the saloon at a table large enough to seat eight or nine, though Mac and Crane were the only diners.

As Slocum approached, Mac motioned him over with a fork that held a bloody chunk of steak.

"Sit, sit, my young friend," Mac said, waving the hunk of steak in the direction of a nearby chair.

Slocum took a seat, meeting the cold gaze of Crane head on. "Probably heard, I've been robbed over at the hotel," Slocum said.

"Nothing happens in this town I don't hear about," Mac answered, finally putting the meat into his mouth. "Most times I hear about it before it happens."

"Don't suppose the sheriff caught those fellas?"

"Sorry to say, the scoundrels got away clean," Mac answered as he chewed.

"They took all my damned money," Slocum said. "Didn't leave me with nothing. Not a damned thing."

"I'll thank you not to curse at my table," Mac answered, still chewing. "But under the circumstances, I can wholly see where the temptation to profanity is understandable. Quite understandable. Just the same, I won't abide it. Not at all."

"You planning on doing anything about it?" Slocum asked. "Or just sit there and talk manners like an old biddy at Sunday School?"

Just then a waiter appeared at the table.

"Bring this boy a steak," Mac said, motioning to Slocum with his empty fork. "Make him up a nice dish, I expect he's hungry after the little nap he had."

"Yes, sir," the waiter answered and vanished.

"Now, where were we?" Mac said, cutting off a chunk of meat and spearing it with his fork up to his mouth. He seemed to accomplish this in one neat gesture.

"I was asking if you planned on doing anything about it," Slocum said. "Seeing as you hold yourself up to run things here in town and all."

"Fortunes of the West, I'm sorry to say," Mac answered. "I'm quite certain you can understand that."

Just then Crane spoke up, his voice as flat and cold as a sheet of ice. "Mr. Mac's a busy man. He ain't got time to worry 'bout your piddling stake. He got himself a town here to run, or ain't you noticed?"

"That piddling stake was all the money I had," Slocum said.

"I like you, boy. Have I told you that?" Mac said, chewing. "I truly like you."

"That don't put money in my pocket," Slocum answered.

"And money is what you need," Mac said, laying his fork down on the plate and bringing up a linen napkin to dab at his lips. "Money is what we are discussing here, isn't it?"

"That's what I thought we were discussing," Slocum said. "My money."

"Boy, you ain't got any money," Mac shot back.

"You got less than no money," Crane added. "You owe money. You got some real problems."

Slocum sat there dumbfounded, letting the idea sink in.

"Mr. Crane, I presume you have the list?" Mac said.

"Yes, boss," Crane answered and pulled a small piece of paper from his pocket and handed it to Mac.

"This here is your accounting as of this morning," Mac said.

"Two days at the hotel for you. Two days at the livery for your animal. Doctor charges. And, of course, the meal you're about to eat. Comes to a nice piece of change. Not counting the pennies, 'bout twenty-five dollars."

"Who all do I owe it to?"

"Me," Mac said instantly. "You owe me money."

"Why, you old bastard!" Slocum swore.

"I'll thank you to refrain from profanity," Mac said calmly, his fat fingers resting lightly on the table. "I won't ask you again. I don't like it, not a bit."

"I know, it means a weak mind," Slocum said. "But I've been hit on the head and my stake stolen. So maybe my brain ain't working like it should."

"As sure a sign of moral turpitude as any I can think of," Mac said. "I do not indulge in profanity myself and will not tolerate it in others."

The whole idea of arguing over a few cusswords while every penny Slocum had was riding East, West, North, or South, was nearly ludicrous. But Slocum knew, too, that the old bird had something planned. "What is it then?" he asked.

"What is what, boy?" Mac answered as he began cutting into his steak again.

"You're gonna make me some proposition," Slocum said. "Some kind of arrangement, ain't you? That's what this whole deal is about, isn't it?"

The waiter brought Slocum's steak then, setting the large plate down in front of him, then vanishing quickly back into the kitchen.

"A deal, you say?" Mac answered. Then added, "Eat up, boy. Nourish yourself."

Although Slocum's appetite was fading fast, he cut into the steak, releasing a flow of bloody juices from its center.

"Now, hear me out," Mac said. "You owe me money. I went out and saw that animal you got over at the livery. Pretty animal. I'd give you twenty dollars for her and another five for the saddle."

"She's worth twice that," Slocum answered. "Just her, she's worth more than twice that. My outfit is worth five times that, you thievin—"

"You find anyone in town willing to pay your asking price, then you take it," Mac said, chewing a hunk of meat.

"But seeing as you run the town, I don't suppose I will, will I?" Slocum asked, bringing his own forkful of meat to his mouth. He knew now that it was better to stay calm and see what the old codger's game was.

Mac shrugged. "This town isn't rich," he said finally. "Folks here, they're just barely getting by as it is, without having to buy an expensive animal like the one you got for sale."

Slocum chewed slowly, enjoying the taste of the steak despite himself. "I doubt they'd buy it, anyway," he said at last. "I mean that would keep you from stealing it and all. Isn't that right?"

"That's a piece of conjecture you'd do well to forget," came the answer. "You can sell me the animal right now. And start walking for Carson City. You got that bill of sale for our friend here, Mr. Crane?"

Crane dug into his pocket again and pulled out another slip of paper and laid it on the table.

Slocum made no move toward the bill of sale. "Or, you got another proposition, isn't that right?"

"Ah, what a bright lad you are," Mac said, overjoyed, around a mouthful of steak. "I told you so, didn't I, Mr. Crane. I can spot these things. You'd do well to remember the lessons I'm teaching. Prove invaluable in business."

"Yes, sir," Crane said flatly as he eyed Slocum with cold suspicion.

"My proposition, as you put it, is this," Mac said. "I still have that piece of river than needs panning. If you're willing and able to do the work, I see no reason why I shouldn't stake you."

"Stake me, how?" Slocum said, wanting to make certain he had more of the details.

"I give you equipment, supplies, and the right to pan on my claim," Mac said. "Whatever you pull out of that river comes back to me and will be used to pay off your debt."

"Less, your share for the right to work the river," Slocum said.

"You are a bright lad," the old man said. "Half is my

share, the other half pays your debt and for equipment and supplies.''

"Might take a bit of work to pay it off," Slocum answered.

"Take more than that to get your sorry hide over to Carson City with no horse or supplies," Crane put in.

Mac ignored his employee. "That's my offer, sir, take it or leave it," he said. "I've offered men worse deals and haven't been turned down."

"I don't suppose you get turned down very much, do you?" Slocum replied. Despite himself, he could feel the bitterness creeping into his voice. The old man had him over a barrel. He knew damned well he was being shanghaied on dry land and didn't care much for it. But every way he looked at it, he saw he didn't have a choice. He had to take the old man's deal.

"Is it a deal then?" Mac asked.

"You got yourself a deal," Slocum answered.

"Good then, I'll see you first thing in the morning and we'll draw up the contracts. And eat your steak boy, after all, you're paying for it. Expect you'll work some for your money, too."

"I expect I will," Slocum answered, cutting into the hunk of meat.

"Before I forget the matter entirely, Mr. Crane here does have a piece of good news for you," Mac said.

Slocum waited, wondering just what piece of good news Crane could offer.

"They dropped this on their way out," Crane said, reaching into his belt and pulling out Slocum's .44. "Wouldn't like to see any man without a gun."

Slocum took the proffered side arm and slid it smoothly into the holster. "Suppose you just figured it was convenient to forget about it until we made our deal, is that it?" Slocum asked.

"Never like talking business to an armed man," Mac said. "Man with a side arm, especially if he knows how to use it, maybe he feels like he has some confidence. A little power, as it were. I, myself, always prefer negotiating with unarmed men, as a matter of policy, you understand."

"That's about the first thing today I do understand," Slocum answered.

5

There were four of them to see him off the next day. Crane and three other men, all of them mean, loafed in front of the livery as Slocum packed his supplies on the mule that Mac had supplied. The mule and the supplies, right down to the last strip of dried beef, were all accounted for in a ledger.

"That mule, that's a damn fine fit for you," Crane said, watching Slocum secure the supplies to the beast.

"I could just keep going," Slocum answered, pulling the rope tight.

"Going? And where would you be going? Carson City? Virginia City maybe? Hell, maybe you'll just jump on up and hightail that mule into a fine hotel in San Francisco."

"What's to stop me?" Slocum asked, already knowing the answer.

"I'll stop you, all right. Remember that," Crane said.

"Keep thinking on it. As a lawfully sworn deputy of Paradise, I'd be in the law if I shot you. Hell, there ain't much I can't do to your sorry hide that's against the law. Keep thinking on that."

Slocum led the mule out into the sunshine by the halter. The four men followed close behind. "How many men Mac got working for him?" Slocum asked, dragging the mule's head in the right direction out of town. The head moved reluctantly, though the remainder of the animal stayed put.

Crane spat and grinned. "Hell, boy, everybody in Paradise works for Mac," he said. "You ain't figured that out yet?"

Slocum pulled harder, but the beast refused to move. "What about mining?"

"Twenty men up there, panning," Crane said. "Every ranch below, every piece of hay cut down, it's all Mac's. Get used to that idea. He owns you, boy."

Slocum pulled hard and felt the dried halter about to snap. "He don't own me," Slocum grunted, still pulling at the mule.

Off to the side, Crane's men snickered, enjoying themselves at the expense of Slocum's hardship with the mule.

"Owns you as much as that damned mule," Crane said and gave the beast a hard kick in the haunches to get it moving. "Me and the boys'll be stopping by the camp. Just a neighborly visit, you understand."

"Don't expect no pie and coffee," Slocum called over his shoulder bitterly as he walked the beast out of town.

As he made his way down the one street, he became keenly aware of the people. Store clerks, ranchers, and farm women all watched his humiliating progress in an attitude of knowing despair.

He had just walked a little way beyond the last structure in Paradise when he saw it. The house was built up on the hill, far back in the shade of trees. Not a big house, but wholly out of place. A small winding trail had been cut through the trees, and it was well worn. It led in a series of sharp switchbacks up to the house.

Smoke curled from the stone chimney, but that was not what held his attention. What caught his eye in particular were the women. Stationed on the porch were four or five women, standing like sentinels.

Slocum kept his head turned toward the women as he continued on, and in return, they watched him with more than casual interest. He knew what the house was, but didn't figure Mac to be much of a whoremonger.

When he was nearly beyond the trail, he turned the mule and began making his way up to the house. Maybe, he thought, he could trade some coffee or biscuit fixings for something that would keep him warm with the memory while he was working off his debt to Mac.

The girls on the porch seemed to brighten a little at his approach. One or two of them smiled cautiously, as if they didn't expect too much. When he was nearly to the clearing in front of the house, one of the girls vanished inside.

"Howdy," Slocum called in the friendliest voice he could manage.

One of the girls, a plump thing with skin as white as dough, said, "Howdy, mister."

He was in the clearing now, feeling foolish holding on to the mule's halter with one hand and taking his hat off with the other. "How you ladies doing today?" he tried.

"We're just fine, better than most, I 'spose," one said coyly.

Just then, another woman came through the front door, followed by the one that had stepped inside a few moments ago. "Mister, if you ain't got money in your pockets, then you best keep moving," she said.

Slocum saw that she was a tall woman, a little older than the others, but better looking by far. She wore a modest dress that Slocum guessed was store-bought in a city and had her reddish brown hair done up fashionably on the top of her head. She wasn't the kind accustomed to work. Slocum took her for the boss. "I figured on trading," he said.

"Trading what? Some of Mac's wormy beef, I suppose?" she answered with a sneer.

A couple of the girls tittered, but quieted quickly enough to hear his answer.

"You girls are about the prettiest thing I've seen in an age," he said. "What's say I trade this mule."

"He ain't yours to bargain with," the woman answered. Then to the girls, "You get back inside. You're showing this man something he can't afford."

The girls obediently filed back into the darkness, every one stealing a glance over her shoulder. Slocum would have liked to think it was disappointment that made them look back, and he wouldn't have been too far from wrong.

"You charge for looking?" he asked.

"Mister, I'd charge for thinking about it if I could," came the answer. "Now, you turn that thing around and keep walking."

"Don't suppose you'd spare a fella a cup of that coffee I smell," Slocum asked.

She eyed Slocum hard then, sizing him up. "You don't smell no coffee, but I guess I can put some up," she answered at last without taking her eyes off him.

"I'd be obliged," he said, leading the mule to a post just in front of the porch.

When he had tied the mule, he stepped up on the porch and followed the woman in. "Name's Kate, Kate Douglas," she said, striding through the parlor where the whores sat and giggled among themselves.

Slocum slowed his step to nod to the girls, causing more giggling.

"Coffee's the only thing I'm offering," Kate said, as she opened the door that led into the small kitchen.

Inside, the kitchen was warm and smelled of just-eaten breakfast. The scents of ham, sausage, fresh bread, and coffee hung heavy in the air.

Slocum took a seat at the table and watched as Kate put another big pot of coffee on, carefully measuring the coffee into the pot. "Mac don't own this place?"

"Only damn thing in town the old bastard don't own," Kate said, moving toward the table. "How'd he come to own you?"

"Got robbed at the hotel," Slocum said. "Owed him a little and I'm planning on working it off."

"That's about right," she said. "But I'll tell you, you ain't never gonna work it off."

"Month, maybe two," Slocum answered.

"In a month, maybe two, you'll owe him just as much," she said. "I'll promise you that."

"So that's the way it is, huh?"

"The way it is, the way it's been, the way it's gonna be until someone kills him," Kate said. "I've seen men ride in with a full poke, and happy to leave walking away with the clothes on their backs."

She approached the table and sat opposite Slocum. He could see now, she wasn't just prettier than the girls in her employ, she was beautiful. Her clear hazel eyes were full of the fire of challenge. "How'd he come not to own you?" Slocum asked, just to be asking something.

"This land and 'bout sixty acres on both sides, they're a land grant from the government," she said. "A gift from an admirer from when I lived in San Francisco."

"The government admires you, does it?"

"One particular member, anyway," she said without a hint of coyness in her voice. "One particular married member."

"And Mac?"

"His boys are up here every second week of the month," she said. "We tolerate each other, for now."

Slocum was about to say something else, ask another question, when he heard a commotion coming from the front parlor. Instinctively, he came out of his chair, hand on the grip of the .44.

"Damn boy, you just can't do nothing right, can you?" one of Crane's men said as he burst through the kitchen door.

"You get out of here, Quint," Kate said. "I'm giving him coffee and then he's moving on."

"Mr. Crane sent me to make sure he finds his way outta town," the stranger said. He was big, with a broad face and a nose that rested nearly flat across his face, it had been broken so many times. He had a full four inches and maybe forty pounds on Slocum.

"I'll move on after I visit awhile," Slocum answered.

The man balled his hands into fists and Slocum recognized the white scarring along his knuckles as belonging to someone who spent time bare-knuckle boxing. "He's going to be moving on now," Quint spat.

"I don't want no trouble," Kate shot back.

"No trouble at all, Miss Kate," the big man said and reached out fast to grab a fistful of Slocum's shirtfront.

Slocum came up faster, knocking the meaty fist away.

The big man's expression changed in an instant from a moist smile to a grimace. Suddenly, his left fist shot out with a speed that surprised Slocum.

Ducking as best he could, he took nearly the full force of the blow at the side of his head and felt his feet begin to slide out from under him as he fell back. Luckily, the table broke his fall, and he pushed off as Quint let go a fast right.

Slocum was ready for the punch this time. He ducked and danced a little to the left, feeling the force of the punch sail by his ear. Then he countered with a fast right, catching the big man full in the gut. It was like punching the trunk of a tree. The big man took the punch and didn't move.

Slocum punched out again, this time with his left fist, striking Quint in the arm. The blow deflected a blow aimed at Slocum's head. Now Slocum moved in fast, bringing his knee up between the big man's legs. He connected solidly with a force that raised the man off the ground and sent him stumbling back.

"Sonofabitch!" Quint gasped as he went for his gun.

Slocum advanced quickly, catching the man's gun hand as the big Navy Colt came out of the holster. Bringing his knee up again, he caught Quint on the wrist and he heard the sound of breaking bones, like stepping on dry twigs.

Quint let out an animal yell and the gun fell from his grasp. Slocum twisted hard, grinding the broken wrist at the joint and sending Quint to his knees, gasping.

"Now I'm gonna have my damned coffee," Slocum said, as he brought the man's arm up and then down hard across the baker's table, busting it at the elbow.

"You're a dead man, you bastard," Quint gasped through the pain.

"You didn't hear what I said?" Slocum hissed and brought the arm up again quickly, this time pulling it from the shoulder socket.

Quint gasped and cursed as Slocum held his full weight on the mangled arm. A second later, Slocum twisted Quint's arm yet again, then released it so Quint was on his back with the arm splayed up behind his head at an impossible angle.

"Now, I'm gonna have my visit with these ladies, then I'll be on my way," Slocum said.

"You're a dead man," Quint gasped, rolling to his side.

"Get up and get out," Slocum answered.

Slowly, the big man rose to his knees, then gained his feet, the arm hanging uselessly at his side.

The girls who had gathered at the door, now feigning shock at such violence, moved aside for him as he staggered through the parlor and out onto the porch.

"Mister, you just bought yourself and me a world of

trouble," Kate said. "Best thing you could do now is take off out the back and keep going."

"I'll think on it," Slocum answered, sitting back down at the table. "I'll think on it after I have that coffee you promised me."

6

"Coffee? Why the hell not?" Kate said, moving toward the stove. "If I die, I should be awake."

Outside the kitchen's door, the giggling of the girls had ceased. The whores were now talking in excited voices. The sound reminded Slocum of birds before a storm. "He's going to call Mac down on us, is he?"

"I'd bet on that," Kate answered, pouring a stream of thick, black coffee into a pair of blue metal cups. "Question is, what Mac's going to decide to do to us."

Slocum accepted the cup she held out and stared. She seemed unusually calm as she took a seat across from him at the large table. "How'd he come to own this town, anyway?" Slocum asked.

Kate took a sip of the steaming coffee, her eyes studying him above the curve of the cup's rim. "I came here, five, no seven years ago," she began. "I was married then. My

49

husband, he was a geologist. Figured we could maybe take enough out of the river to get a stake for a ranch. That man was crazy for cattle. Know what he used to say?''

Slocum shrugged and took a sip of coffee.

''He said, 'At the end of the day, a rock's a rock. Big or small, it's a rock. But a cow—that's beauty in a leather sack.' I wouldn't be lying if I said he was an odd man.''

''And he found the gold?''

Kate took another sip. ''It was just where he said it was going to be. He said we'd find silver; we found gold. He put in the claim and the next thing we know some railroad speculators—part of a so-called syndicate—came to us. Two fellas, one fat and one skinny, both of them in derbies. Seems they were planning on putting a light rail system against the side of the mountain. They were buying up land down both sides of the mountain. Our claim was right in the middle. My husband made a deal with them. Government gives us the land grant and we sell to them, to fill in that last piece at the end.''

''That way it would be quiet,'' Slocum said. ''Instead of them going to the government directly.''

''Crooked deal from the start,'' Kate answered. ''But there was another syndicate interested in the route.''

''That would be Mac, right?''

''Not him,'' Kate chuckled. ''He ain't really nothing but a clerk, but tell that to the folks out here. People he works for, they're all back East. But it was him, he tried to buy us out, and when that didn't work, he and his men killed my husband and tried to run me off.''

The talking outside in the parlor had lowered to a hush. Slocum could hear the slight rustling of dresses and knew that at least five ears were pressed against the door, listening to a story the girls had more than likely heard a hundred times before. "And the other syndicate?"

"They got scared off and bought out," Kate said. "And I'd bet you dirt to dollars nobody was shooting at them, that none of them died. Probably just got scared they'd lose money or something."

"And when they came back, Mac's bosses, you still didn't sell, right?"

"You're a smart fella," Kate said. "I lost my man to them sonsabitches. I wasn't about to give, sell, or trade nothing with them. That was a good man they killed. Smart, too. That land grant was two hundred acres of solid land. They can't build no railroad, light gauge or nothing, without it. There won't ever be a railroad built on this land."

"What's to keep them from killing you?" Slocum asked after a long drink of the strong coffee.

"I got a will drawn up by the best lawyer in San Francisco," Kate said. "If I die, the land goes to two women who had their husbands killed by Mac's boys. And they got wills, same kind as me, that gives it over to two more women. It goes on like that, right down to the children."

"What's keeping you here, then?" Slocum asked.

"Land grant," Kate said. "Original holders of the land got to live on it. That's part of the deal."

Slocum turned the situation over in his head. The whole you setup began to make sense. "He's just figuring on waiting you out, is that it?"

"That's it," Kate answered, meeting Slocum's steady gaze. "He figures I'll give up after a year or two. And when I do, they get the land with a town already built."

"That little parlor trick at the hotel, stealing my money. Mac pull that often?"

"Every chance he gets," Kate said. "He gets 'em any way he can. Hell, he got twenty, thirty men, women, and children up in the hills pulling gold out for him. He got ranches down below breeding cattle, and farms growing his grain. And he sets the price on every damned thing. Old Mac, he sets the price and owns the notes on what folks owe. He ain't interested in nobody getting out of debt."

"And if any of them start saying they ain't going to pay or try to run—"

"His boys beat 'em or worse, just to teach the others a lesson," Kate said, then added, "or he sets the law on them. He owns every animal in town. A man rides out toward Carson, even if it's on the horse he rode in on, he's a horse thief. It ain't the way the law was supposed to be, but that's the way it works in Paradise."

Slocum drained the last of his coffee and stood up from the table. "I guess I should be heading out now," he said. "If I bring any trouble on you, I'm sorry."

Kate hunched over her coffee and shrugged. "He can't do nothing to me," she said. "Hell, half his men are sneaking up here every chance they get. For them to do anything, it would be like biting the hand that feeds them."

"Hand?" Slocum asked with a smile.

Kate returned the smile, her face brightening for a moment. "Maybe not the hand," she said. "But they seem to need and enjoy it."

Slocum returned her smile, not sure what to say.

"I'll tell you what. Why don't you just lay down for a spell," she said. "Think about what you're going to do.

You head up to that camp, they'll kill you. You go back to town, they'll kill you. You try running to Carson, they'll kill you or put the law on you.''

There were three rooms on the upper level of the house. These rooms, Slocum supposed, belonged to the most favored girls. Out back, there was a long, crudely constructed shake divided into three partitions, which the less accomplished girls used to entertain their customers.

"This one is my room," Kate said, opening a door to a room at the front of the house. "You can bed down in here till dinner."

It was a small, neat room, containing a small bed, a chest of drawers, a bookcase packed with technical manuals, and a table that held a lamp and washbasin. What caught Slocum's eye in particular was the Henry rifle propped against the window.

"I know how to use it," Kate said, following the line of Slocum's gaze. "Haven't had much practice, but with you here, I probably will."

"You'll hit them before they leave town," Slocum said.

"It'll make a mess of a man," she said, then took a tentative step forward. "Fella sees his pardner hit with that, it makes him think."

Slocum moved forward, meeting Kate in the center of the room. "Have I told you I appreciate your hospitality and all?"

"You told me, but you ain't shown me," she answered.

A moment later she was in his arms. He held her tightly, feeling her shallow breathing and the warmth coming from the bodies through their clothes. Reaching a hand up slightly, he undid the pins that held her hair and let it tumble down in a rich cascade.

And then they were kissing, their lips joining hotly together. From that first kiss, Slocum could tell that she was just as hungry for lovemaking as he was.

When they finally broke the kiss, Kate's face was flushed and she was breathing harder. Their eyes met, and he saw her hunger there. "Got to close the door," she said, turning in his arms and reaching out to shut the door. "Don't let anybody ever tell you there's any privacy in a whorehouse."

As he kissed her again, she brought her body in close, rubbing against him as the stiff shaft under his canvas pants grew hard. Awkwardly, they half-stumbled, half-fell across the bed, their arrival announced by the creaking of springs. An instant later, their hands were working frantically at each other's clothes.

With each article of clothing that he removed, Slocum feasted his eyes. She rolled on top of him, straddling him at the waist and worked at his belt as he pulled the material of her dress and underthings down in a gentle motion.

It had been a long time, too long, since he had a woman. And now, as Kate's full, firm breasts with their thick red nipples came into view, he felt as if he were a starving man suddenly set before a banquet table.

As she finished with his belt and began working buttons drawn taut over his manhood, he reached up and guided one of her breasts toward his mouth. Kate let out a long, low moan as Slocum worked his tongue around the already hard nipple. Then gently, very gently, he began teasing it with his lips.

Kate arched her back and brought her hands down to massage his hardness through the trousers.

When he had finished with one breast, he let it gently slide from his mouth and took in the other. Again, he worked his tongue slowly, teasingly around the nipple. A low purr, like a cat, came up from her throat and through half-parted lips. She bent toward him, offering more of the milky whiteness of her breast, and a waterfall of hair tumbled down across his face. "I've been meaning to treat myself to something," she said in a husky whisper. "And you're a damned lot better than a new dress."

Poised above him with her dress pulled down to her waist, Slocum had to admit that she was about the best thing he'd seen in a long time.

Then, as if she'd reached some decision, she turned and worked her way quickly down his legs. At first he didn't know what she was doing, but she grabbed one boot and pulled it off and then the other.

"Nobody comes to bed with their boots on here," she said, tossing the boots across the room. Turning again, she was now straddling him just below the knees. Bending, she finished working at the buttons of Slocum's trousers. He raised himself slightly, allowing her to pull them down and freeing his now throbbing shaft.

"Oh, yes," she purred, her hungry gaze fixed on the shaft, "a damned lot better than a dress."

Slocum reached forward under her dress and felt the wetness there. Slowly, he allowed his fingers to play against the moist undergarment so that they traced the outline of her honeypot. She moaned again, shutting her eyes and grinding herself down on his teasing fingers.

Gently then, he worked his hand into the top of the undergarment. She was not wearing a corset. The flat stomach and straight back were entirely her own. When he felt the first damp touch of her, Slocum let his fingers curl in the fine silken hair and tease along the wet slit.

"I'm ready, now, please," she moaned, grinding down even harder in a small circular motion.

"I reckon you are," he answered.

She raised herself slightly then, drawing her undergarment down along with her dress. For a brief instant, she was nearly standing high over him, and when she lowered herself again, she was naked.

Reaching out, she grabbed his shaft gently, letting her fingers play along its sensitive underside, then she raised herself up slightly, guiding it into her.

Slocum let slip a low groan as she brought herself slowly down and engulfed him in moist warmth. For a moment they remained perfectly still, savoring the first taste of their pleasure. And then she began to move, her hips working in smooth, slow circles.

Slocum raised up at the hips, burying himself deep inside her and then bent forward. She, too, leaned forward and for a moment his face was buried between her firm breasts. Reaching up with two hands, he slowly began massaging her nipples with his thumbs. When she leaned farther toward him, he again took her breast into her mouth, this time sucking hard at the firm nipple.

Soon they were moving faster, and the old iron bed complained with every thrust. Slocum released the breast from his mouth and reached down to massage the place between her legs with a thumb.

A quiver of excitement spread through her, then he felt her clench his rod hard inside her. Wave after wave of pleasure was released from some secret place deep inside her and she cried out as her fingers dug deep into his shoulders.

A second later, he felt his own release and heard a voice he recognized as his own moan loudly as he thrust upward, his shaft burying itself completely inside her.

7

Slocum awoke alone in the dark room to the sound of piano music. He lay in bed for a long time, wondering if he had really slept the entire day. When he decided that it was a possibility, he began to smile. It was Kate, he knew, who had worn him out with her lovemaking.

Slowly, he brought his legs off the bed and began hunting around the darkened room for his clothes. When at last he found his trousers, he pulled a lucifer from the pocket and lit the small lamp on the bedside table. After washing his face and just generally trying to make himself as presentable as possible, he ventured downstairs.

The second he entered the parlor, the piano music stopped. The young whore, hands poised over the keys of the small instrument, turned toward him, offering a hard stare. Four other whores, dressed in robes and underthings, sat on the sofa and stared as well.

"Kate here?" he asked in what he figured to be his most pleasant voice.

The whores continued to stare, then looked away, their arms folded across their chests.

"Good day to you too, ladies," he said, touching his fingers to the brim of his hat and pushing through the kitchen doors.

It was in the kitchen that he found Kate. She was sitting at the large table, her hand curled around a cup of coffee, staring into a spot on the wall. From all indications, the wall was infinitely fascinating, certainly more interesting than Slocum.

"Something wrong?" Slocum asked as he approached the large table and Kate.

"Nothing that a bullet in Mac's brainpan wouldn't fix," she answered.

Slocum took a seat directly across from her and said, "He sent some kind of word back about that fella this morning, didn't he?"

"Three men," Kate said. "They rode up while you were sleeping this afternoon. Said they passed a law against the house that afternoon in a council meeting. I didn't even know the town had a council. Hell, we ain't even in the town, officially. But that don't matter."

"It won't last," Slocum said. "A week, maybe two, Mac's men will be tomcatting around up here. You'll see. Those laws never amount to much."

"It ain't the law I'm worried about," Kate answered. "Right after those men showed up, another of them came in. Said that Mac said any man caught in here is to be shot. That there's the unofficial law. That's the way Mac works.

He passes one law out in the open and makes up another unofficial law.''

"What are you going to do?" Slocum asked, studying her face for some clue. What he saw bothered him. All the strength she'd shown earlier was gone now.

"I won't risk none of the girls," she said. "It ain't worth it. Those are good girls out there. They've been unlucky maybe, but that ain't no reason to risk them to Mac's men."

"What are you going to do?" Slocum repeated, feeling himself hunch forward a bit over the table.

Kate turned her eyes from the wall to Slocum for the first time since he entered the room. "Hell, I got a little money," she said. "Enough to buy them train tickets and give them a little extra. That'll have to be enough for them. One or two was talking about Carson City, Virginia City. Another one has people she can go to in Chicago. I'm not risking them to no gunplay. They don't deserve it."

"They want to leave?" Slocum asked.

"They don't know what they want," Kate replied. "A couple of them's been talking nonsense about taking on Mac and his men and getting the other ones all worked up over it."

"They're grown adults," Slocum answered in a low voice. "If they want to fight, you should let them."

"If they want to get killed I should let them?" Kate snapped. "All together they don't have a bit of sense between them."

"This is their home, ain't it?"

Kate stared at him long and hard, her gaze fixing on him where he sat. "Slocum, this is a whorehouse," she said, her voice just barely calm. "And it ain't even a very good whorehouse."

"Let me ask you this," Slocum said. "Are you leaving? Are you packing up and going about your way?"

"Looks like I'm gonna be moving soon," Kate said. "After the girls leave, there's nothing stopping Mac and his men from setting the place on fire. A penny's worth of coal oil would send me living back in town working for Mac."

Slocum thought about it for a long time. Kate was right. After she sent the girls away there was no doubt in his mind that Mac and his men would just set the house ablaze. After that, Kate would move back to town and Mac could figure some other way to steal the property from her. "You pay that money I owe to Mac and I'll stay on," Slocum said.

"Stay on for how long?" Kate asked. "Just 'cause you bedded me doesn't mean I got to trust you."

"Stay on for as long as it takes," Slocum answered. "Stay on till it's all over."

Kate snorted at this piece of news and offered him the type of smile you'd give a not-too-smart child. "It ain't gonna be over," she said. "It won't be over until either Mac gets the land or he dies."

Now it was Slocum's turn to smile. It was a small, sly smile. "See there, that's just what I was talking about," he answered.

"You'd do it, wouldn't you?" she said in not much more than a whisper. "You'd be just dirt-dumb enough to take that bastard on."

Slocum nodded, still smiling.

"Him and his twenty, twenty-five men," she said, a little awestruck. "You'd take them all on, wouldn't you?

"And how much would you want to be paid for this?" Kate asked. "That doesn't mean I'd pay it, I'm just curious like. I want to know how much you're willing to get killed for."

"I'd do it for what I owes him," Slocum said, his voice even and calm.

Kate seemed to freeze there for a moment at the news, her mouth coming open slightly as she stared. "Let me get this straight," she said at last. "You're planning on paying Mac back what you owe him—what he stole from you— so you can kill him?"

"Yes ma'am," Slocum said, enjoying her disbelief more than a little.

"And this makes sense to you?" Kate asked, coming forward on the table to hear the logic by which Slocum arrived at his unusual plan.

"The way I see it, if I kill him now, people will say I did it 'cause I owed the money to him," he began. "They'll say I killed him to avoid paying what I owe. Maybe they wouldn't even say it, but they'd think it. And they'd be right in thinking it."

"But if you pay and then kill him?"

"Then they'll know I killed him 'cause he's a dirty son-ofabitch," Slocum said. "After I pay, he'll be coming after me, you can count on that. And folks will know he was a crooked bastard. And not just folks in town, either."

Kate continued to stare, the logic of his reasoning running through her brain. "You're a strange man," she said at last. "Don't know if I like dealing with such a strange one, but I figure that I'm gonna have to risk it.''

"We got a deal then?''

"Hell, why not?'' Kate answered.

"So, when are you gonna tell the others?'' he asked.

"Tell the others?'' she said, a bit startled. "Hell, this is a whorehouse, there ain't any secrets in a whorehouse, or haven't you learned that yet?''

It was true. As soon as she said it, Slocum could hear the distinct sound of giggling and the rustling of robes coming close from the other side of the door. The girls had been listening since Slocum entered the kitchen.

The next morning at sunrise, Slocum harnessed the team to the surrey and brought it around to the front of the house. The girls, all five of them, dressed in their best finery, were waiting on the porch.

Kate stepped from between them and offered her hand to Slocum so he could help her into the front seat of the wagon.

"They're all going?'' Slocum asked, as he continued to help them up onto the cracked leather seats. "Mac's men are sure to be there.''

"That's the whole idea,'' Kate said. "Let them and the rest of the male population of Paradise have a little look at what they'll be missing because of their new law.''

Now it was Slocum's turn to agree with Kate's logic. But it wasn't being in town that worried Slocum. It was the ride to and from town that had him concerned. If Mac's men were going to start any trouble, it would be on the small stretch of switchbacks at the far end of town where they would plan it.

As they started on their way, the girls in the back giggled and opened parasols. Behind the wagon, packed as neatly as the day before, was the mule that Slocum had led up the trail.

It was not a long ride, but at every turn, Slocum imagined that he could see Mac's men in the trees on the hillside above them. If someone was going to ambush them, it would be before they reached the town.

Heads began turning as soon as they entered the town. Slocum couldn't blame the miners and store clerks for staring. As the wagon passed, they froze in their tracks, their eyes following the wagon down the street. After all, it wasn't every day that a surrey packed with whores and leading a mule came into town.

By the time they reached the saloon, the wagon had made enough of a mild commotion to draw Mac himself out on the boards to welcome them. He stood there looking plump and prosperous with Crane at his side.

"You have wounded one of my men," Mac said, removing his morning cigar from his mouth.

"It was a fair fight. He tell you that?" Slocum said, still holding the reins.

"He was in no position to say much of anything," Mac answered. "You made him useless to me now. I fear he'll have to find another line of work."

In answer, Slocum threw down the leather pouch with the coins in it. The pouch flew through the air and landed at Mac's feet. Mac made no move to retreive it.

Slocum was gratified to see that more people were gathering on the street to watch the encounter, but remained silent.

"And what is this?" Mac asked, letting the pouch hold his attention for only a second.

"What I owe you," Slocum said. "It's all there; count it."

Mac made a slight motion with his cigar and Crane bent to pick up the pouch. "What you owe me?" Mac said.

"Count it," Slocum answered.

"And that mule, you'll be returning that, I take it?"

"And taking my horse," Slocum replied.

Mac opened his hand and Crane put the pouch in it. A small smile spread across his face as he felt its solid weight. "Then, may I assume you'll be leaving us?" Mac said.

"I found a job," Slocum said. "I figure on staying on awhile."

Mac put the pouch in his pocket and took a long pull on the cigar, thinking. "A job now," he said, letting out the blue gray smoke into the morning air. "If I may inquire, what sort of employment would trash like you find in Paradise?"

"He's working for me, Mac," Kate said, speaking now for the first time since they entered town.

"Morning, Kate," Mac said. "I suppose you've already heard of our new town ordinance."

"You know I have, Mac," Kate said. "You sent that trained dog up, didn't you?"

Mac smiled wider, well aware that people were listening to the exchange. "I was only allowing myself the certainty that you were fully apprised of the situation," he said. "As for Mr. Slocum here, it seems he chose the wrong time to join your little establishment. Though I wonder in what capacity he ever intends in serving. Even in the West, untamed as it may be, surely we have not become that loath-some.''

This comment drew a small chuckle from the crowd.

Slocum, not wanting to prolong the conversation for any longer than necessary, stepped down off the wagon and untied the mule. He led the beast around the wagon and secured him to the post in front of Mac.

As he was securing the animal, Mac said in the smallest of whispers, ''You're a dead man. You hear me, you ungrateful creature?''

''A pleasure doing business with you,'' Slocum said in a clear loud voice and tipped his hat to Mac and Crane before climbing back up on the wagon.

8

It was much to Slocum's relief that the girls in the back of the wagon didn't cause any trouble as he pointed them out of town. From what he could see, they busied themselves with whispered talk and nodded politely in the direction of some of their more regular callers. The men, some of them with their wives, ignored with embarassed denial the polite nods and small "howdies" the girls offered. That's the way it was with whores all over. During the day, the men didn't want to know them. But come night, they'd be knocking on the door and staring at the ground.

Nevertheless, Slocum guessed that more than one of them would have some serious explaining to do when they got back to the ranch or the mining shack that they called home.

"All things taken into account, I think it went rather well," Kate said as they moved beyond the town's last buildings. "Don't you think?"

"What I think is, we ain't heard the last of Mac and his boys," Slocum answered. "What I'd like to know is what they're planning now."

"Course we ain't," Kate answered matter-of-factly. "It wouldn't surprise me any if he's sent some of his boys along to finish the job now. That would be the smart thing to do. End it quick like. Send a couple of his men up in those trees there with a rifle or two. Just blow you right out of this wagon."

Instinctively, Slocum's eyes followed the trees, looking for movement. He half expected to see the long barrel of a Winchester sneaking out among the branches or the brim of a hat between the leaves.

"Course then, he'd risk hitting one of these ladies," Kate added, smiling. "At the very least, spraying her with brain and blood. It would be enough to put a girl off her work. Her heart wouldn't likely be in it with her Sunday dress splattered with some drifter's brain. I can't think of anything that'd spoil a mood quicker. Can any of you girls?"

A few of them said "nope" from the back of the wagon while the others just giggled.

Slocum felt himself relax a little with the logic of it, but bristled just the same. He didn't like being played for a fool any more than he liked Kate joking about him getting his head shot open over a whore's Sunday dress. "Is that what they put into their work, their hearts?" he said. As soon as the words were out of his mouth, he could feel every woman in the wagon stiffen.

"Now, there wasn't no reason to speak like that," Kate said. "None at all."

"I apologize," Slocum answered, really meaning it, particularly since, if Kate was right, the women riding behind him had more than likely saved his life. Turning, he saw them nod, accepting his apologies.

"Let me tell you something about the business I'm in," Kate said. "Out here, you or nobody else doesn't want to do a blessed thing to upset these girls."

"I understand that," Slocum said.

"You get just one leaving, it's going to give the others ideas," Kate continued. "Pretty soon, one, then two, then you got the whole pack of them moving on. You got them thinking of Chicago or San Francisco or some damned place that ain't here and you got trouble."

"I understand that, too."

"Now, Mac and his boys, they understand that," Kate said. "This is what I've been thinking lately. That is, they want me off that land in a bad way. But they don't want me gone altogether. He may talk like a preacher to the married ladies, but the minute these girls start packing bags, he's got trouble with every man in his town that ain't married, I can promise you that for sure. I figure that to be about half."

"So he don't want you out altogether?"

"Hell no," Kate spat. "Well, maybe me he wants out, but he sure don't want these girls out. Not that he'd ever admit it. Hell, he'd build some shacks up on the hill, away from the wives and such. Build some shacks and get one of his boys to run it. Imagine what that would be like?"

"I wouldn't do nothing for him, nothing," one of the girls spoke up suddenly.

"Course you wouldn't, Charlotte," Kate said. "Nobody said you had to, did they?"

"I just wanted it known," the girl replied in little more than a whisper.

They continued on in silence, the landscape passing slowly before them. Slocum was lost in thought. Only now was he putting together the pieces of what he'd gotten himself into. For years, Kate and Mac had been in a standoff. More than likely, if neither of them had forced their hand, it would have remained a standoff for a bunch more years. Mac was too afraid to move on Kate, and she was too damned stubborn to leave.

But then Slocum had arrived and tipped the scales in Kate's favor. Despite all the men Mac could arm on a word, Slocum had upset some natural balance between the two. He had no doubt, none at all, that there would be bloodshed.

"What are you figuring on doing?" Kate asked, sitting down at the kitchen table.

All the girls had vanished as soon as they reached the house. Some, he suspected, had retreated to their rooms to sleep, unaccustomed as they were to being up during the day. Others were occupying themselves with old copies of magazines.

"I can't say," Slocum said, taking a seat opposite Kate. "You got any ideas, I'd be glad to hear them."

"You got to go after him, you know that, don't you?" Kate said, staring Slocum straight in the eye. "You leave now, he'd send men after you. If you left, you better not think of sleeping till you reach Texas."

"I ain't leaving," Slocum answered, taking what Kate said as a threat.

"You going after them, then?"

Slocum made a point now to return Kate's hard stare. "How do you figure I do that?"

"One at a time," Kate said. "Find yourself some hidey-hole in town, pick 'em off as they come out of that saloon. Fella like you, that shouldn't be any problem at all."

"What kind of fella do you figure I am?" he asked.

"The kind that doesn't mind killing, if he knows he's in the right," Kate said flatly. "The kind that knows that sometimes killing's the only way to stay in the right and keep on breathing."

Slocum pretended to think it over, though he already knew the answer to what Kate was asking him to do. "Let me tell you something," he said finally. "The minute I put a bullet into one of those men, the second I dry-gulch even the worst of them, I'm in the wrong. I'm in the wrong before they hit the ground."

"I'll tell you what I know," Kate answered suddenly. "I know that a coward's always in the wrong. And that's what you're starting to sound like, nothing but a coward."

"I ain't a coward, but I ain't no hired gun, either," Slocum replied. "You wanted a hired gun, you should have bought yourself one. There's plenty enough of them around. They work cheap, too."

A profound look of sadness came over Kate. She looked away slowly, her eyes turning to study a spot on the floor. "Men, you're all a sorry damned lot," she said. "You're all hellfire willing to shoot each other up over a two-dollar poker hand. That's nothing to you. You'll draw down on each other for an insult, for a lie, for one of them girls sleeping yonder. But when something's at stake, something real, you stand aside like a bunch of damned preachers and clerks.''

"You don't understand," Slocum said, though feeling that she understood a whole bunch more than he was willing to admit, even to himself.

"What don't I understand?" she said, turning her eyes up suddenly on him, pointing them at him as if they were two gun barrels. "Whyn't you just tell me what it is that I don't understand?"

Slocum met her challenge, but moved on. "How many men you say he's got?"

"Hell, he's got the whole damned town," Kate answered. "Every man in town. Ain't a man in town that don't come running when he hollers for them."

"How many paid out of his pocket?" Slocum asked. "How many to do his dirty work for him?"

"Sixteen, twenty maybe," Kate said. "The rest, they maybe get something off their accounts if they do what he says, that's all."

"How many guns do you figure he's got?" came the next question.

"A dozen that are any good," Kate said, her tone softening now with hope. "But they're good. He got them from all over, Texas, Kansas, Arkansas. They're mean. The one you took care of, he wasn't the meanest of the bunch."

"If I took care of them, what would he have?" Slocum asked, not yet knowing why, but only that it was important that he knew.

"That wouldn't do no good," she answered. "He'd only

get more. Mac can order them up like a mail-order suit. Like you said, there ain't no lack of them and they ain't what you'd call expensive. Not to Mac, they ain't.''

''But that first dozen, what would happen if I took care of them?''

''If you did it before he could get more, he'd be through,'' Kate said. ''The others, that weren't so good with a gun, they'd make themselves scarce, I can promise you that. They owe Mac money, not their lives.''

Slowly, a plan took shape in Slocum's brain. Even before he saw the whole thing, he knew what he had to do. The only thing he didn't know was how he was going to go about it, but he was sure he'd think of something.

''What are you thinking?'' Kate asked. ''And why the hell are you smiling like that? You haven't gone idiot on me or some damned thing, have you?''

''Haven't gone idiot on you,'' he said, still thinking, letting the idea take hold on its own.

''Then would you mind telling me why you're grinning like a damned idiot?''

''Do I need a reason?'' Slocum asked, still smiling.

''I'd say that you damned well better have one,'' came the answer. ''What with the mess we're in, I'd hate to think I was depending on a grinning fool.''

9

Slocum headed out before daybreak. He left before the air was touched by the thin blue of dawn and when the night chill with its dampness could still be felt through his heavy coat. He saddled his horse in silence, rousing the animal from sleep and whatever dreams its brain could conjure to pass the night.

He took nothing from the house, not even a biscuit, and left his saddlebags behind. Still, he could imagine the first few minutes when his departure would be noticed. The girls would roll out of their beds sleepily and reluctantly and make their way into the kitchen. Kate, no doubt, would be right behind them. It wouldn't take long before they discovered him gone from where he had spent the night in the parlor. Perhaps for as long as an hour they would think that he departed forever. They wouldn't even be mad and the anger they released and their curses would be just for show.

Of course, they would know him to be like any other man who takes what he pleases.

Perhaps this would last an hour, perhaps two, until they discovered his saddlebags and the clothing in them. For if there's one thing that a whore knows, it is that of all the things men leave behind, clothing is not on the list.

These are the things that the big Southerner thought of as he rode steadily up into the hills, nudging the horse under him in reluctant progress forward. Soon the horse moved of its own accord, working its way higher into the hills with steady surefootedness.

As the first light began to filter down through the trees, Slocum found what he was looking for in the two sets of tracks that marred the old Indian trail at a fork. Even in the dim light, he could make out the markings of a mule and a man. Slocum climbed down off his animal and knelt beside the tracks. From the look of them and the way they were spaced, the mule was loaded down with supplies. The man was walking alongside, probably pulling it along by the halter.

Slocum followed the trail on foot for a quarter of a mile, noting the way that in some places the man seemed to slip at the effort of pulling the beast along. Slocum judged them to be no more than a day old and to be the last to use the trail.

Climbing back on his horse, Slocum began to follow the tracks in earnest. They moved straight ahead, not departing from the trail. Two miles or more from where he first spotted the tracks, Slocum spotted a small stream. It was here that the tracks moved from the trail, through a tangle of brush, and into the stream.

Pointing his horse off the trail over the brush already crushed by man and mule, Slocum began to follow the stream uphill. The stream was pebble-bottomed and shallow. Slocum's horse had no trouble keeping its footing.

As they moved along, walking slowly against the swift current, Slocum kept his eyes moving from one side of the stream to the other, looking for a break in the brush. He didn't want to risk missing the miner's camp, though he suspected that would be almost impossible the way they were heading.

Almost a mile upstream, the water ended at the face of a stone wall and a small waterfall. To the left was a large clearing into which the mule and man tracks led and to the right the dense green of pine. Slocum reined his horse to the left and entered the clearing with one hand raised high in case someone was watching his approach.

When he was near the center of the clearing, a voice said, "That's far enough. I don't care if you do work for Mac, I got a shotgun on you."

"I don't work for Mac," Slocum said, looking toward the brush in the direction of the voice.

"Ha! That's a damned joke," the voice answered in a bitter laugh.

"I don't work for him, not anymore," Slocum answered.

"What's your business up here, if it ain't to do with that bastard?" the voice said. "Tell that sonofabitch I'll have his money come Sunday, just like always. Or did you follow me up to charge me for breathing, is that it?"

"I said, I don't work for him!" Slocum insisted.

Suddenly the brushes in the direction of the voice trembled and a shotgun, followed by a man, emerged. The man was maybe thirty and gaunt. He had sandy blond hair and the big, raw bones of a farmer. But the thing that held Slocum's attention were his eyes. The man had a pair of pale blue eyes that had a haunted look to them. "What's your business then?" he said, keeping the ancient ten-gauge raised at Slocum. "I told that bastard if he sent any more of his killers up here, I'd blow 'em in half. I warn you, I'm one to keep my word."

"I'm taking my gun out," Slocum said. "I'm gonna reach for it."

"Reach for it slow, like," the man said, coming forward in a stooped crouch.

Slocum let his free hand drop down slowly and he extracted the Colt from its holster with two fingers. Then he held it in front of him for a moment, offering it out.

"Just throw it yonder here," the man said, motioning slightly with the shotgun.

Slocum was beginning to question his own wisdom for coming to the place. For all he knew, this man was crazy. He'd seen panners before that went crazy from being alone for too long. But he knew he had to risk it. "I ain't gonna throw it," he said. "You want it bad enough, you come and take it."

The man approached slowly, cautiously, as Slocum held the Colt out. Then, when no more than the shotgun's barrel stood between the two, the man reached out quickly, like a bird, and grabbed the Colt.

"Be sure not to drop that," Slocum said, watching the miner stuff the gun into the knotted length of leather that served as his belt.

The miner looked up from the gun, his face beaming with

triumph. "Now, why'd Mac send you?" he asked. "Better answer quick and true. Shooting you is no more to me than shooting a wood rat."

"I told you, he didn't send me," Slocum answered.

"Then why'd you come?"

"You work for Mac?" Slocum asked, knowing already the man did. "How much you owe him?"

"None of your business," the man spat back over the shotgun's barrel. "That's between me and him."

"Let me ask you this," Slocum said. "How much do you figure you took out of here?"

"Plenty, I'll tell you that," the miner said, smiling a mouthful of busted teeth. "I took plenty out of the stream. Cold mined it, I did. Panned it and dug it. I took plenty out. Once I get squared, this claim is mine. I get the papers, whole deal."

Slocum could see now that the man was crazy. But he wasn't crazy like you see miners, not with greed, anyway. "How'd you like not to work for Mac?" Slocum asked.

"What's that? You're talking crazy, mister!" came the sharp response. "You talking like a crazy man. Mac owns this. Mac owns the mountain. Ain't nothing around that he don't own. I'll tell you this, you come up here to cheat me out of my gold, you'll be the sorriest sonbitch alive. I'll tell you that. Mac'll call the whole damned army in. That's right, whole damned U.S. Army. Blow your sorry ass off his mountain. Off my gold."

It was no use talking to him. Slocum could see that now. The miner had dug and scrapped and panned alone for too long. Probably he hadn't seen gold of any kind in quite some time. "That's fine then," Slocum said. "I think I'll be moving along."

"You best be," the miner said, smiling with triumph again. "I seen you yesterday, talking to Mac. Seen you throwing gold at him. Who you kill for that? Mind telling me that?"

"I didn't kill anyone," Slocum answered and motioned for the man to hand back the Colt.

"And you ain't going to, neither," the man said. "Not without a gun, you ain't."

"Mac ain't going to like it, once he hears about you robbing folks up here," Slocum said. "Can't imagine that would sit well with him."

The miner seemed to think this over, his brain working feverishly and his eyes going flat with the work. "And if I give it to you?" he asked, finally.

"I'll be on my way," Slocum said. "I'll ride out of here like nothing happened. Just like we never met."

"What'll you tell Mr. Mac?" the man asked, his concerning growing now.

"Nothing," Slocum answered easily.

"Tell 'im that I aim to own this mine in a month, maybe two," the man said. "Would you tell him that? Would you tell him I can smell it? I can smell the gold under there. Do you understand how a man can do that? Mr. Mac can, I know he can, 'cause he's the type that puts his brain to working on something and it happens. Would you tell him that?"

"Sure," Slocum answered. "I'll tell him that."

The miner hesitated for a moment, then withdrew the gun from the waist of his baggy trousers. He handed it up to

Slocum, grip first, the way he had received it. "Now, you just get on out of here," the miner said. "Go back and tell Mr. Mac what I said."

Slocum nodded cordially and turned the horse.

It was midmorning now, the sun sliding up into the sky. As Slocum retraced his steps, he thought of the insane miner. The way that fear and greed had come together in his eyes was oddly unnerving. Slocum had seen crazy people before. The good Lord knew there was no shortage of them. But the miner was a different sort.

By the time he returned to Kate's house, the girls were all up and about. Two of them busied themselves sweeping off the small front porch, while two more were engaged in feeding the chickens. They tossed the grain out haphazardly, causing the half dozen chickens to run first to one end of the small yard and then the other.

Slocum unsaddled the horse and secured it in the small barn out back, then made his way into the house through the kitchen. Kate was sitting at the table, her hand curled around a cup of coffee.

"You have yourself a nice little ride, did you?" she asked without turning.

"Interesting, anyway," Slocum said.

Kate turned now, slowly. "I know you didn't go into town 'cause you ain't dead."

"Rode up into the hills," Slocum said. "Found one of Mac's miners."

"Yeah?" Kate answered, now interested, as her eyes followed Slocum from the small stove where he found the coffee still warm to the narrow counter where the cups were set out.

Pouring himself a cup of coffee, he said, "Man was crazy."

Kate seemed to snort, then said, "Which direction you ride?"

"East and a little north," Slocum said, then took a sip of coffee. "Followed a stream into the hills."

"Four or five miles from here?"

Slocum nodded.

"That would be old Ned," Kate said. "He's crazy. Crazier than most of them."

"Mac takes money from him?"

"When he comes into town, which ain't that often," Kate answered. "He's been up there almost since the beginning. Mac probably forgets about him when he ain't around. About six, seven months ago, he shot at a couple of Mac's boys that was just riding through. Didn't hit nothing, but Mac's let him be since then. He's crazy and Mac knows it. The hired guns know it. Everyone in town knows it. If he wasn't crazy himself, Ned would probably know it."

"So Mac just lets him be, is that it?"

"He isn't hurting nobody up there," Kate said. "He comes to town, buys what he needs out of what he scrapes out of that creek, then heads back."

"They're not all like that?" Slocum asked. "All the miners?"

"One way or the other, they all are," Kate said. "That's the pity. They're all looking for gold, scared of Mac, and Lord help anyone who tries to stand in their way."

10

Slocum slept the remainder of the day in Kate's room. It had, by any accounting, not been a tough day, but the failure of his attempt to deal with the miners had left him weary. It was that and the fact that he had somehow fallen under the spell of the whorehouse. In just a day or two, the clock on which the house ran, which was counter to the schedule of farmers, ranchers, clerks, and all manner of honest working people, had somehow infected him. Oddly, he found himself craving the night.

He awoke sometime just before supper, as the last rays of the sun came slanting in through Kate's bedroom window in colors of dying feeble gold and red. He lay in the bed a long time, his eyes open and without a thought in his head. But somehow that was enough. The bedroom smelled of Kate and of the harsh soap and cheap perfume she used. And it smelled slightly of their lovemaking the day before.

As he was turning over some notions in his head, the door opened and Kate stood there. "Well, you're going to start earning your keep today. I want you downstairs in ten minutes," she said, and left without waiting for his answer.

For Slocum's part, he didn't see where he had a choice. He had failed in his attempts that morning and now he was at Kate's beck and call.

After rising slowly, nearly painfully from the bed, he washed in the small basin and dressed, making sure to put on his cleanest dirty shirt.

When he entered the parlor, he saw that Kate had a few customers. Two young men sat on the parlor sofa talking to the girls. They looked to be ranch hands, no older than twenty or twenty-two. They were big, gangly boys with eager smiles and an attitude of overstated politeness. Both held their hats in their laps and nodded, smiling as two of the girls talked to them.

Slocum offered the group a quick "howdy" and moved off to the kitchen, barely noticed.

Kate, dressed in a bright red dress, was busying herself at the stove. "Not bad, at least you're good at following instructions," she said, not turning toward him. "Just maybe I wasn't throwing good money away on you."

"Now that I'm down here, what is it you want me to do?" he asked.

"Just make it known you're here," she said. "In case there's any trouble."

"From them?" Slocum asked, motioning toward the parlor. It was unlikely either of the youths would cause a lick of trouble, their thoughts being occupied by other concerns, namely picking out a girl for their evening's pleasure.

"Not them," Kate said, turning toward him now. "Hell, those boys are from down country. They probably haven't even heard of the fuss you caused yet."

The sound of one of the girls giggling echoed from the parlor, followed by the sound of footsteps as she led one of the lads to a room.

"But they will," Slocum said. "Someone's bound to tell them soon enough."

"You're right there," Kate said, leaning back along the wall near the stove. "And when they do, then I won't even have their two dollars anymore. What I'm asking you to do is just be a man around the house when we do our business."

"Man around the whorehouse, you mean," Slocum answered wryly.

Ignoring his comment, Kate said, "I don't think Mac will try anything just yet, but you never know with him. Just keep ready for trouble. That's all I'm asking you, is keep ready for any trouble that shows up at that door. You figure you can manage that?"

"Shouldn't be too hard," Slocum answered. "You want me to stay out there with them, is that it?"

"Hell no!" Kate shot back. "Nothing makes a customer more nervous than some man leaning and moping around a whorehouse parlor with a long face. If he's wearing a brocade vest and an eighty dollar New Orleans suit, that's one thing. But if he looks like a gunslick or saddle tramp, well, it's liable to put customers off a mite. You understand that, don't you?"

"You're saying I don't have what it takes to be a fancy man?" Slocum asked, feigning insult.

"Mister, I don't know what you got," she said. "I just don't want you in the parlor scaring the clients away. Come on now, I'll fix you some coffee."

There were a few other customers throughout the night. Mostly they were farm boys and hired hands, riding into town for a little fun. If any of them heard about Mac's wanting to shut the whorehouse down, none of them mentioned it. But then, what could Mac offer them that was more appealing than a two-dollar roll with a somewhat pretty girl? And what could he threaten them with that would be in a young man's thoughts when his blood began to rise and he took a hankering to sleep with something softer than his bedroll?

It was a losing battle that Mac was waging against the whorehouse. Unless he could contrive to get every eligible man married and bedded down with a wife, then he'd be fighting nature every inch of the way. That's the way Slocum thought of it. Because he knew that a whorehouse is just as much an act of nature in a small town as floods, droughts, and the passing of the seasons. It's as if they were planted upon the landscape by some invisible hand with the same predictable regularity as snowfall and the changing of the seasons.

When the last of the customers had tipped his hat at the door and vanished into the early dawn, Slocum took a seat in one of the parlor's chairs and stretched out his legs.

Kate, pushing through the door of the kitchen, saw the last girl off to bed and joined Slocum in front of the small fireplace. "Well, that's the last of them for the night," she said, stretching her feet out as well.

"You have a good night?" Slocum asked, talking just to be saying something.

"Sixteen dollars," she said. "I've seen some better nights, and a bunch that were a lot worse. This one here, it was about average. That's all I can say for it."

"So you don't figure on Mac and his men hurting you none in the business end of things?" Slocum said by way of answer.

"Too soon to tell properly," she replied. "I don't know if he's tried yet. He could just be sitting back thinking of some mischief."

They sat alone for a long time, each enjoying the silence. Finally, Slocum stretched and yawned. "I think I'm going to be turning in," he said. "Just so I know, where am I sleeping tonight?"

Kate smiled. It was a sly, catlike smile. "Come on, I'll show you," she said, getting up and leading him by the hand to her bedroom.

They were barely behind the closed door when she approached him quickly. "Sometimes I get downright jealous listening to them girls work those beds all night," she whispered hotly in his ear.

He took her in his arms, drawing her even closer as she began to unbutton the front of his shirt. When she had all the buttons unfastened, she kissed his strong, firm chest.

Then Slocum gathered her into his arms and brought her feet off the ground. Taking the two steps to the bed easily, he eased her down and climbed in next to her. "I know what you mean about them beds," he said, as he began to work at the small pink ties that held the front of her dress together. When he had undone two of the ties, he bent and kissed the pale, soft flesh at her throat, feeling it tremble slightly under the touch of his lips.

Slowly, inch by inch he began working his way down, letting his lips linger across her skin. Soon, her entire body seemed to be trembling, her full lips slightly parted, then opened wider to let out a small moan.

He began working at the tiny buttons that fastened the remainder of her dress. When he had them completely undone, he reached down and felt the firm calf muscle of her leg and let his hand glide slowly upward. As he reached the edge of her underthings, he slowed, gently letting his fingers work at the ties that held her knickers to her waist. When he had these unfastened, he worked the tips of his fingers down from the top, feeling her wetness as his fingers reached their destination.

"Oh, yes," she moaned as he let one finger trace a teasing line up and down the center of thatch, turned moist with desire.

Ever so slowly, he worked his finger in to where it was smooth and slick. Kate arched her back, moaning, as she tried to fill herself with his finger.

"Easy, easy," he whispered. "Make it last."

"Damn you," she said, half cursing, half laughing. "Oh, damn you. Please."

Slocum worked his finger up and down slowly, finally letting it slide nearly completely into her.

Kate let out a moan and wriggled as she brought her arms up to wrap around him. She held him tight, her fingers stiff as she dug her polished nails into his back.

And then Slocum withdrew his finger. A second later, he was shrugging out of his shirt as she worked frantically at his belt. He knelt next to her and she pulled his stiffened shaft from its place, grabbing it from the underside as she slowly stroked it.

"Oh, it's lovely, lovely," she cooed, admiring his shaft in the faint dawn glow coming through the window. Lust had made her eyes more catlike now. They were nearly slits with a fire burning in them. "Bring it over here. Please, please."

Slocum rearranged himself so that he was now straddling her as she continued to stroke his long, hard member.

"Closer, closer," she moaned, drawing him up as she pulled on the shaft.

Slocum obliged and a second later, the thick, hard shaft was an inch from her lips. She continued stroking with one hand as she deftly pulled down her light shift from her shoulders, freeing her two large breasts.

Rising slightly and arranging herself on the pillow, she took the head of his throbbing member into her mouth, gently drawing it in as if she were breathing. Still stroking it from the underside with one hand, she let her tongue slide slowly around it.

Slocum reached one hand back and slowly, gently slid a single finger inside her. And when she moaned, he could feel the sound she made up and down the entire length of his shaft. As he began working his finger in and out of her, her tongue repaid him a thousand times for the effort as she took the entire length of his shaft deep, deep within her mouth.

And then, when his shaft was wetted down to her satisfaction, she released her one hand from it and placed it between her breasts. Rising up a little more on the pillow, she then took her two hands and crushed her breasts against his member, completely enclosing it in her delicious warmth.

"Oh, that feels so, so very good," she purred and took the head of his member into her mouth again.

Slocum began working his hips then, gently driving the length of shaft into her mouth and slowly pulling it out where it glided between her two breasts.

Soon the furrow between her breasts was as warm and wet as where he was working his finger.

He worked his shaft slowly at first in short, tentative strokes. But very quickly, he could control himself no longer. Soon, he was working it in and out of her mouth and between her breasts in long, quickening strokes. The member would dive deep into her mouth where that fantastic tongue would seemingly play over every inch of it, then draw it out between her two warm breasts.

Very quickly, she began to moan again and he could feel her tightening around his finger. As he felt himself approach release, he began rubbing her small nub with the side of his hand.

She moaned again at the first touch of this secret place and raised herself against his touch. He drove his member hard into her as she reached release and felt an explosion as her mouth filled and the place between her breasts became even wetter.

When they were finished, Kate held him in her mouth for a long time. Her tongue idle now, she released her breasts and waited until the proud shaft was no longer hard.

Slocum rolled off, settling into a soft place beside her as he took her into his arms and they both drifted off to sleep.

11

It seemed as if Slocum had only been asleep for a moment when a frantic knocking at the door startled him from his slumber. Kate sprang up at the same instant.

And then there was the voice of one of the girls. "Come quick, please," came the cry. "Something's happening! Mac's up to something!"

Slocum and Kate sprang out of bed at the same instant. They reached the door together and Slocum flung it open. The girl was standing there, twisting her hands together. "They're up to something. Come see!" she cried.

"Where are they?" Slocum demanded, already moving past the girl, the Colt in his hand.

"There!" she cried. "Out, down by the road!"

"Start talking sense," Kate demanded, holding the girl by both shoulders. "What's going on?"

"I was out, down by the road, and I saw them," she

said. "The wagons, there must be fifty, a hundred of them!"

Slocum dressed hastily, pulling on his pants and stepping into boots. Halfway down to the road, he was still buttoning his shirt. Kate was right behind him, lagging no more than two or three steps. If there was something to see, he wanted to see it.

Half falling as he ran down the hill, he heard the sound of wagons before he saw them. And then, as the trees thinned out, he saw them. The girl had been right; there were a lot of them. More than fifty. Their number, he guessed, was closer to a hundred. Chances are, the first wagons were already unloading in town as the last were yet to arrive. Most of the wagons were covered by gray canvas, but Slocum could see clearly enough that they contained lumber.

"Damn, they must have cleaned out every sawmill between here and Carson City," Kate said, as she came up alongside Slocum.

"You got a sawmill nearby don't you?" he asked, his eyes still fixed on the parade of wagons.

"Just outside, up in the hills. But nothing that could turn out this," Kate said, shaking her head. "Good sized barn would set them to working round the clock."

"Ever see anything like it?"

"When they built the hotel, they hauled it in like this," Kate answered. "Saloon, too. All the rest they took their time, built them slow."

"What do you figure this is?" Slocum asked.

"Could be anything, a chuch maybe, I don't know,"

Kate said, her eyes still on the parade of wagons that passed before them.

They watched until the last wagon had passed. They stood there for a moment in the settling dust that the procession had stirred up, both of them certain that whatever it was Mac had thought up, it wasn't good.

Slocum was the first to turn back to the house. By this time, the other girls had joined them, coming down the hill silently to watch the wagons pass.

"What are you figuring on doing?" Kate asked him, running a few steps up the hill to catch up with him.

"Really, there's only thing thing to do," Slocum answered. "Go into town to see what the fuss is about. It could be nothing."

"I'll get the girls together and you harness the horse," Kate said.

Slocum slowed his step. He didn't much like the idea of hiding behind women. "I'm going alone this time," he said.

Kate came to a halt, forcing Slocum to turn to answer her. She stood a little way down the hill, the girls crowded behind her. "They'll kill you," Kate answered. "Without me, they'll kill you sure as you're standing there."

"They'll try to," Slocum said. "And I didn't much like the way it went last time."

Kate put her hands on her hips. "Didn't like having to count on a bunch of whores, is that it?"

"Didn't like hiding behind women," Slocum answered, and turned to start walking again.

"You'll die owing me!" Kate shouted after him. "You hear that, you bastard? You'll die owing me!"

"Sell the horse," Slocum said, still not turning. "Sell the guns. We'll be even."

Kate and the girls watched him walk up alongside the house to the barn to get his horse.

"You think he's gonna do it?" one of the girls asked in a whisper as they crowded around Kate.

"He'll try to ride into that town, just to show that he can," Kate answered. "And he'll probably get killed for his trouble."

Not more than a quarter hour later, Slocum had his horse saddled and was riding down the narrow trail that led to the road. He didn't have a thought in his head, except maybe to find out what the wagons were about.

He didn't know how, but he felt that whatever they were brought in for, he could use it to his advantage. The miners would prove no help at all. If he were to believe Kate, the ones that weren't outright terrified of Mac and his men were crazy for gold. And when a man is filled with either fear or greed, there's no sense in getting between him and either one of those two things. The two of them, fear and greed, were like two different sides of the same coin. Both of them able to occupy the whole of a man's mind without much room for anything else, whether that be hate or just plain common sense. Both of them were like madness.

Slocum coaxed his horse to a quick walk, and before long he could see the last of the wagons making its way to town. He kept back fifty or so yards, watching the progress of the parade in front of him and thinking what Mac could be up to.

By the time they reached town, there were crowds of

spectators lining the street. They stood on either side of the narrow street, staring as the wagons rode down the center. Small boys filled with courage and curiosity edged off the boards and ran alongside the wagons before being yanked back by a mother or father.

Slocum noticed that as the last wagon in front of him moved before the crowds, the people seemed to drift along with it. And, when it reached approximately the halfway mark of the small street, the first tentative notes of music began. Apparently there was a band on the far end of the town.

Slocum pointed his horse toward the saloon and tied it to the post. There was no sense in making himself more conspicuous than necessary. Walking slowly, he joined the last of the crowd in the curious migration along the main street.

When he reached the end, he stood at the edge of the crowd. Mac was standing on a small, hastily built stage in the center of the street. In front him, standing on the ground, a small band was playing a tune. Behind him, sitting on chairs, were four men, all dressed in suits.

"Friends! Friends! My good friends!" Mac began, holding up his hands. Instantly the band ceased to play.

A group of workmen paid Mac no heed. They were already busy unloading the wagons. Perhaps twenty wagons stood, already unloaded, behind the small stage. A huge pile of timber planking was growing next to the last building on the left. And even as Mac tried to quiet the crowd, wagons emptied of their loads passed in front of the stage, moving in the same direction from which they had arrived.

"Friends! Listen to me and I will explain," Mac shouted,

smiling. "Good citizens of Paradise, you see before you today, our opera house!"

A low murmur moved quickly through the crowd and Mac gave his audience time to digest the news.

"Friends, you see behind me, Preston Crompton, architect from San Francisco, who designed it."

With that, the man directly on Mac's left stood for a brief bow to accommodate the applause.

"And his son, Ned Crompton!"

Another wave of applause swept through the crowd as a younger man stood up.

Slocum, already knowing what was coming next, turned his back to the stage and began walking back down the street. As he walked, the voices from the stage, Mac's and then a voice he took to be that of the architect from San Francisco, grew faint, and he could no longer make out the words.

He was walking down the center of the street and was halfway back to his horse when a voice to his side, said, "Bang."

Slocum turned toward the voice and saw Crane standing next to the post that supported the saloon's overhanging roof. He was standing there, one finger pointing the way a child makes a gun of his hand.

"You're dead," Crane said, then pretended to holster his finger. "Just that easy."

Stopping in his tracks and turning to face Crane head on, Slocum replied, "If it's that easy, friend, maybe you should have pointed something else at me besides your finger."

Crane smiled and shook his head slowly. "Not my

place," he said. "Mac figures you'll be gone soon enough."

"Gone, huh?" Slocum asked, watching Crane's hands, which were now casually resting on his hips.

"Gone," Crane said. "He figures you'll get tired of poking them girls up there and slip out through a window in the middle of the night."

"You mean, once I've had my fill, is that it?" Slocum answered, taking a step closer.

"Either that, or you'll join up with us," Crane said. "I don't see that as too likely. But Mac figures that you're maybe a better hand with a gun than you seem. Myself, I am what you'd call dedicated to making sure that don't happen."

"So, I only got one choice, is that it?" Slocum asked, all the time moving in closer.

"You got two choices. I ain't one to leave a man without any choices," Crane said. "Leave town or die. Both of them are fair choices. All you got to do is decide which one suits you better, is all."

"I'll tell you what, I'll think on it," Slocum answered, stepping right up to Crane. "I'll give both of them some serious thought."

"You do that," Crane said.

Slocum started walking again, this time stepping up on the boards and moving next to Crane before continuing down the boards. For a brief second, he was so close to the man he could smell the cheap barbershop scents on him. As he walked toward where he tied his horse, he could be fairly certain that Crane wouldn't shoot him in the back, not without Mac's say-so and not with so many witnesses so close.

"Ain't you curious about what we're building?" Crane called after Slocum.

"Opera house is what they said," Slocum answered without turning.

"Gonna be a palace," Crane called. "Have the whole shebang up in two days."

Slocum continued on without answering. An opera house made perfect sense as far as he could see. It would give the folks in town something to do besides go to the whorehouse. And, too, there were probably a few rooms in it that could be adapted for that purpose as well, for some of Paradise's more upstanding citizens.

Of course, Slocum knew that Mac could have built a church. A real church is a way to keep folks occupied. Nothing marries off a town's single men faster than a string of church socials. But a real church, an honest one, wouldn't put a penny into Mac's pockets. An opera house was a business he could use to suck more money out of the town and accomplish pretty much the same thing as a church. Mac wasn't a fool. He knew as well as Slocum that many's a man who raised hell in a whorehouse on Saturday night and prayed for heaven beyond on a Sunday morning.

12

"Well, he was liable to do it sooner or later," Kate said. She was on the back porch, tossing feed to the chickens. Slocum noticed how she fed them, thinking about each handful of feed she pulled from the pail and tossing it with care.

"The way I see it, the thing can only hurt you," Slocum said, standing next to Kate.

"It won't help me, that's for sure," she said, tossing out a handful. "But it won't hurt me much. Not as much as he thinks, anyway. His boys and the others, they'll still come tomcatting around, you'll see. And they'll pay enough to put food on the table."

"And what do you think about that other thing?" Slocum asked.

"About what Crane said about you, you mean?" Kate answered slowly. "I don't think he was lying. There's probably a job waiting for you with Mac, if you want it. But maybe not. Generally, I think he doesn't believe you're worth the trouble. Crane, now, he's a different story.''

"He's taking it personal, you mean?"

"Personal, not personal, I believe he wants to see you die," Kate said matter-of-factly. "Maybe he just doesn't like the competition. His boys, they're mean, but they're a mangy bunch. If you came riding in, willing to switch up sides on this thing, I do believe it would give Mac pause.''

"You mean, who could do the job better, is that it?"

Kate stepped off the porch, scattering the chickens as she tossed the last handfuls of grain toward the far corner of the yard. "I believe so," she said. "Knowing Mac, he'd let you two fight it out for the job.''

Slocum turned silent then, thinking of how to use this bit of insight to his advantage.

Kate turned and said, "You ain't thinking of going to work for Mac, are you?''

"You think I could take Crane?" he asked, knowing in his own mind he could, but wanting another opinion, just the same.

"In a fair fight, with witnesses, you could," Kate answered thoughtfully. "I'd have to say that you'd have the advantage there, what with Crane not having a whole lot of experience in fair fights and all. But he's got the men to make sure any fight he walks into isn't fair. What are you thinking on, anyway?''

"Nothing, just thinking," Slocum said, and walked back into the house.

Kate, of course, was right again. The men continued to come to the house. Sometimes they showed up at the back door and sometimes they came in the dead of night, just before dawn. But they showed up, bashful and mumbling with their hats in their hands.

But by the second day, with the wagons still hauling in supplies for the opera house, the men stopped arriving at the door.

"Something's wrong," Kate said late on the third day. "Something's bad wrong."

They were all gathered in the parlor. The girls were decked out in their best robes and undergarments, and had arranged themselves around the room on the couches and chairs. "Maybe someone gave one of them something," one of the girls said. "Word gets around."

"Nobody gave nobody nothing," Kate snapped. "Unless somebody ain't saying. Any of you had any problems?"

All of the girls, eyes on the floor, shook their heads.

"It isn't them, Kate," Slocum said. "It's something else."

"Maybe they got a show going on," one of the girls said. "Maybe we can go."

"They ain't got no show that can compete with what we got here," Kate said. "I want all you girls to try to remember that."

Even before Kate had finished speaking, Slocum pushed himself off the wall and headed for the front door.

"And where you think you're going?" she asked in a stern sneer. "You off to the opera house?"

"Just thought I'd get some air," Slocum answered, stepping out the front door.

He moved quickly, walking off the small front porch and down the trail. As soon as he was out of the yellow lamp glow of the house, he headed for the trees.

There was a bright moon in a nearly cloudless sky and it wasn't hard to navigate himself down toward the road. He walked slowly, taking care to move silently down the gently sloping hill. He knew what he was expecting and saw it as he approached the road.

Thirty yards or so ahead were two men sitting on a log near the side of the road. They were talking casually, their voices traveling up the hill.

Then, as Slocum continued to make his way downward, he heard the sound of a horse. The men lifted themselves up off the log and approached the road.

Slocum hurried down the hill to get a better look at whatever was going to happen.

The horse and rider came to the curve in the road just before the trail up to the house. Both men met the rider with shotguns.

"Where you think you going, boy?" one of the men asked.

"Up there," the rider answered, nodding toward Kate's house.

"No you ain't," one of the men said, raising the shotgun.

"I ain't?" the boy, probably a ranch hand asked.

"Not up there," the other man said.

"I don't reckon you can tell me I can't," the boy said, a cautious anger rising in him.

"Them old whores, they're old enough to be your momma," the first man answered. "You thinkin' on paying some woman you're own momma's age?"

"They ain't," the boy shot back. "And I don't see where it's any of your say."

"It's my say, boy," the second man said. "Now you turn yourself around and head back."

Slocum was right on them then. As he approached, coming silently out of the underbrush, the boy's eyes brightened a little.

"You stupid, boy?" one of the men asked, seeing that the rider had quit talking. "You dumb, you don't hear what I'm telling you?"

"He hears you fine," Slocum said, thumbing back the hammer as he nudged the barrel of his Colt into the man's back. "But he ain't listening."

"This isn't none of your business, mister," the other said, venturing a slow look over his shoulder.

"It's my concern," Slocum answered. "Drop that scattergun. Now."

The man obeyed, letting the shotgun drop carefully to the ground. "You don't know what you're foolin' with here."

Slocum, still holding the gun on the first man, reached around and disarmed the second, pulling the Navy Colt from the holster. "Now, that's my concern, isn't it?" he said, tucking the long-barreled firearm into his own belt.

"We're here by Mac's orders," the first one said.

Slocum bent slowly and picked up the shotgun. "That's no surprise," he said. Then, to the rider, "Boy, you go on now, whereever it was you were heading."

The young man seemed to hesitate for a moment, then rode on up the hill toward the house.

"You're a fool, mister," one of the men said to Slocum. "You don't know what you're getting yourself into."

"I think I got a pretty good idea," Slocum answered, shouldering the shotgun.

"You planning on dying for them whores?" the other asked. "Cause that's the only thing that's gonna happen. You're gonna die for a bunch of whores."

Slocum, ignoring him, asked, "You got horses?"

The first one shook his head slightly.

"Then start walking," Slocum ordered. "I see you two, either of you, alone or together, on this road again, I'll kill you. Believe that."

He watched as both men started the walk back to town, then he retreated back into the trees. He heard their voices a little while later and then the voices died away as they continued their trip.

When he was certain they weren't circling around, Slocum headed back up into the trees. When he reached the barn, he propped the shotgun against it, then kept moving. A quarter mile beyond the house, he reached an old Indian trail set against the side of the mountain that ran parallel to the main road. It was narrow and rocky, but he knew it to be the route that some of the customers had traveled in the past. He knew it also was the piece of land that the railroad wanted to build on.

He followed the trail back toward town, keeping a few yards into the trees. It was rough going on the steep incline, but even from the trees, Slocum could see why Kate's husband didn't want a rail line built on it. The speculators were fools for even promoting it. It would be only a matter of time before the rains coupled with the weight of the rails would collapse the trail. A rail line would last a year, maybe two, but eventually the earth below or above it would give way.

When he was almost to the edge of town, where the trail widened slightly, he saw the second pair. One was asleep against a large stone, the other stood patiently, leaning against a tree, a shotgun cradled in his arm.

Slocum came up on them slow. When he was right on the sleeping man, he curled his arm out and covered the man's mouth as he put the cold barrel of the Colt against his temple. The man jolted awake, his mouth opening to yell against Slocum's palm, but then he thought better of it.

Quickly, Slocum brought his hand away from the man's mouth, then reached down and pulled the man's gun out of the holster. When he had the short-barreled firearm secured, he nudged the man to his feet with the Colt.

"Lyle, what you doing out there?" the man at the road called without turning.

The man with the Colt against his head made no move to answer.

"Lyle, what are you doing?"

"I caught us a fancy man," came the voice behind Slocum, just before the big Southerner felt the barrel of a rifle push hard into his spine.

"Now, you drop that piece," the man behind Slocum said.

"I ain't dropping it," Slocum answered, moving the Colt's barrel down, so that it was right behind the man's ear.

"This here is a Sharps .50. There won't be much left if I pull," the man behind Slocum said.

"There'll be enough left to pull on your friend here,"
Slocum said as he pushed the barrel hard behind the man's
ear.

A second later, the man at the road came down, crashing
through the knee-high brush.

"Do something, please Emmett," the man with Slocum's gun at his head pleaded.

"I hear you, little brother," Emmett answered, his voice
unsteady. "Lyle, don't do it. Don't shoot that bastard."

"You heard what Mac said, I shoot him, clean like, without witnesses, it's worth fifty dollars," Lyle answered,
nudging Slocum with the Sharps.

"You shoot him, you won't live to put it in your
pocket," Emmett said through clenched teeth as he drew
his side arm from the holster.

"You planning on shooting me? Is that it?" Lyle said.

"If that sonofabitch shoots my brother, I got a bullet for
you," came the answer.

"If he pulls that trigger, I won't have to pull mine,"
Slocum said. "It'll go right through me and him, and that's
a fact."

"Lyle, please, don't shoot him," the man in front of
Slocum said.

A terrible silence enveloped all of them. Each one
thought of the odds and judged the consequences of every
possible move. Slocum could practically hear the man behind him wondering if he could get two shots off. He'd
have to be quick to shoot first, then raise the gun and shoot
Emmett. Lyle would have to be quick, but if he was quick
enough, it was worth fifty dollars to him.

13

Finally, the man in front said, "Listen, Lyle, we'll take him back. That'll be worth something."

"I'm not going anywhere," Slocum said. "Besides, old Lyle, he's already started into thinking—"

"Shut your mouth, I ain't thinking nothing!" Lyle shouted before Slocum could get all the words out of his mouth.

"He's started into thinking how fifty dollars three ways ain't as much as fifty dollars one way," Slocum said. "Ain't that right?"

"I ain't thinking no such thing," Lyle said. "Don't you listen to him Emmett!"

"Emmett, please!" the man under Slocum's Colt exclaimed. "Help!"

"He's maybe even thinking that even if somehow you three live and I die, how maybe you two won't reach town," Slocum said. "Ain't that right, Lyle?"

"That's a lie," Lyle said, his voice steady.

Slocum couldn't see Lyle's face, but he knew that it sounded true to Emmett. Even in the pale moonlight, he could see Emmett's face flush with anger and his eyes grow narrow with a newfound hatred.

"You would, you would shoot me, you sonofabitch," Emmett said.

"You're listening to him?" Lyle asked. "He'd say anything—he'd say that pigs fly—to save his own hide!"

"That don't mean it ain't true," Emmett said. "A man could tell a lie and still be saying the truth, you filthy bastard!"

"Takes a special kind of man to kill two brothers for fifty dollars," Slocum said. "A man that would do that would have to be something special."

"He'd have his own place in hell," Emmett said, his eyes narrowed to slits aimed at Lyle. "And I reckon I know just what a man like that looks like."

"Emmett, don't listen to him," Lyle said, his voice almost pleading. "He's got you thinking all wrong."

"A man that would do that would dry-gulch some poor bastard sheepman up in Montana, wouldn't he?"

"What you thinking?" Lyle said. "You were there! You were with me!"

"Man that would shoot two brothers would cut some poor drunk in Carson, I'd say," Emmett continued. "He'd be the kind of man that would brag on it. Brag on all his evil."

"You were there," Lyle said, pleading openly now. "You did them things, too."

Slocum could see Emmett curling his finger tighter around the trigger. His face was no longer flushed with hate, but had grown very white the way a piece of iron in the fire grows white with more heat.

"I was there," Emmett said. "I did them things, too. I'll admit to them. Maybe I'll answer for them in the hereafter."

Lyle seemed to relax a little at the confession.

"But there's a big difference between you and me, Lyle," Emmett said. "From where I'm standing, there's a world of difference."

"What? What's that Emmett?" Lyle asked, his voice once again frightened.

"I ain't the one with a Sharps pointed at my brother's back," Emmett said, raising his gun slowly.

As soon as the words were out of the man's mouth, Slocum dove forward, putting all his weight on the man in front of him. As both of them fell to the ground, he kicked up with his boots, the heels hitting Lyle square across the shins.

Above him, Slocum heard two shots thunder together. And when he looked up, he saw Emmett spin to the left as a bullet from the big Henry rifle nicked his arm.

Slocum scrambled to his feet, holding the gun on Emmett. Glancing behind him, he saw Lyle, his left eye a bloody mess. The shot had gone in and not come out. He almost looked like he was sleeping. He sat, strangely restful, his feet splayed out in front of him.

"Damn, I didn't want to shoot him," Emmett said.

"Well, you did a fair job of it," Slocum answered.

"What you gonna do now?" the other brother said, getting to his feet.

"Give me the gun," Slocum said, moving toward Emmett.

The man surrendered the firearm and Slocum added it to the two others in his belt. Then he said, "You hurt?"

"It's something, but it ain't bad," Emmett answered.

"You and your brother, you start walking," Slocum said.

"We got horses up a little ways, up in them trees," the brother said.

"We could head back to town," Emmett said. "Tell Mac you shot him."

"You gonna tell Mac how I shot him with a .38?" Slocum answered. Then raising his gun, "This Colt ain't a .38. That is, unless you're figuring on telling him the truth."

"I reckon that wouldn't be the thing to do," Emmett answered.

"It wouldn't be the healthy thing to do, no," Slocum said. "You and your brother, you get out of here. Now."

"Mister, you ain't leaving us no choice," Emmett said, sadly.

"I'm afraid I ain't," Slocum said, suddenly aware of how strange the scene had become. If things had gone differently just a few minutes ago, these boys wouldn't be talking so politely. They'd be leading a horse back to town with Slocum's body tied down across the saddle. More than likely they'd be joking and kidding each other about who would be able to drink more with whatever extra money Mac saw fit to give them for their trouble.

"I just want you to know, this here was a good job you're putting us out of," the other brother said. "Work like what Mac gave don't come around that often.''

"I'm sorry to hear that," Slocum answered. "But you boys just keep riding south."

"And?" Emmett said.

"And when you reach Texas, you'll find work."

"Not like this," Emmett said.

"Maybe better, maybe worse," Slocum answered. "Now get going."

He watched the pair as they headed for the trees, making their way up slowly. He didn't think either of them carried a hideout, but he couldn't be absolutely sure, so he watched them.

A few minutes later, both brothers reappeared, leading their horses down the hill. The younger of the two brothers led what could only be Lyle's horse. It was a pretty clay-bank.

Slocum noticed that neither had a bedroll. It was likely that everything they owned was back in town; bedrolls, saddlebags, and a change or two of clothes. But even as they headed forlornly down the trail, Slocum didn't let it bother him. Boys like that would always be able to find work.

When he was certain that the brothers were not returning, Slocum dropped the guns he'd taken from them and sat down on a rock to think. The dead man was only a few feet away, his eyes staring up sightless at the new day's sky.

If the brothers hadn't taken the dead man's horse, Slocum would have put the body over it and made sure it got back to town. As it was, he was standing more than a mile from the house with a dead man. He supposed that he could carry the body back to the house, heft it over his shoulders like a deer. But then what?

No, it was better to let Mac think that all three of them had run off. If he judged his man right, Mac wouldn't give it a whole lot of thought. Run off or killed, it was all the same to Mac. All he would think about was how he had three less men. Maybe he would think on it awhile and maybe he wouldn't give it a second thought. Soon though, Mac would send word out on the stage that he needed more men. He would have them sent from wherever it is people like Mac hire men to do their dirty work. He would order them like a mail-order suit. There was never any shortage of men willing to do whatever dirty piece of bidding they'd been hired for. And more often than not, they sold themselves cheap.

After a few moments of thinking, Slocum bent to the dead man and grabbed one of his wrists and a leg. Straining slightly, he managed to get the man across his back and started into the trees. After a little while, he found what he was looking for. There was a narrow gulley, not too deep, where the spring runoff from the hills came through. Just now it was bone dry.

Slocum lowered the body to the ground near a substantial deadfall. Using his back, he pushed the log to the center of the gulley, leaving an impression in the ground where the log had been. Then he rolled the body into the impression.

It took him another hour or so to gather enough rocks to cover the body. He piled the rocks over the corpse until he was certain that whatever critters came along would have to work for their supper, then he walked back up the small hill.

Heading back to the road, he thought briefly of hiding the guns as well, but then he thought better of it. He could be pretty sure that Mac's men wouldn't search hard enough to find the body and maybe railroad him into a murder charge.

When he found the guns where he'd left them, he jammed the revolvers into his pants and shouldered the shotguns and rifle. He felt like a damned fool walking through the trees armed like he was going to war, but the more he thought on it, the more he believed that they just might come in handy, should Mac take to waging war on the whorehouse.

By the time he returned to the house, Kate was the only one still awake. She was sitting at the kitchen table, leaning over a cup of coffee. "I see you had yourself a busy night," she said, as he leaned the rifle and shotguns against the wall and pulled the pistols from his belt and set them on the table.

"Interesting, anyway," he answered, turning toward the stove to fetch himself a cup of coffee.

"How many of them you kill?" she asked, her voice as casual as if she were talking about varmint hunting on a Saturday afternoon.

"What makes you think I killed any?" Slocum answered, turning from the stove to face her with a cup of hot coffee in his hand.

"Most men get that look on their faces after they just killed someone," Kate said. "Kind of mean and proud and scared, all at the same time. It's like they did something and they still don't know what to make of it."

"And I have that look?" Slocum answered, suddenly

aware of every muscle in his face.

Kate studied him for a long time, her beautiful eyes searching. "I have to say, you don't," she answered at last. "You purely don't. And I'm not all that sure if I like that or I don't like it."

Slocum took a sip of his coffee. When he finally spoke, he tried to make it sound casual, as if they were maybe talking about someone else. "Then what makes you think I killed anyone?" he asked.

"For one thing, all those guns," Kate said, nodding at the side arms that rested on the table. "Men in this part of the country don't give up their weapons so easy. Most times they're what you would call downright reluctant to part with them."

"And for another thing?" Slocum said, then took another sip of his coffee while he waited for her to answer.

"For another thing, you got enough blood drying on your back to make it look like someone's been chopping chickens on it," she said at last.

Slocum turned slowly, trying to catch a glimpse of the blood that had leaked from the dead man's eye when he put him over his shoulder.

Kate offered him a small, not what anyone would call happy smile. "How far you have to carry him like that?" she asked.

"Not far," Slocum said. "Not far at all."

"Just as long as you didn't leave him lying in the road, nobody'll notice too much," she said. "That's the way it is in Paradise. It's what you might call the town motto."

"What's that?"

"If it ain't seen, nobody notices," Kate said. "If it ain't seen out on the street, well, it's just as if it don't exist."

14

For nearly a week, the house grew busy again. Apparently, Mac was not a man to play a losing hand. When his plan to put his boys up on the road to head off customers to Kate's didn't work out, Mac simply gave up on it. Money wasn't exactly pouring in to Kate and her girls. But the two or three men who came up the hill for their pleasure seemed to be enough to keep them all happy.

"We ain't getting rich," Kate said one night after the last of the men had left, "but we ain't going to end up in the poorhouse, neither."

"That's all you can hope for," Slocum said, turning down one of the lamps in the parlor.

Kate, still sitting on a thin-legged chair, gave him a harsh look. "I could hope for a bunch more than that," she said. "But that's what I'll settle for, and believe me, it's a good ways less than I ever expected to come away with in this life."

"What life is that?" Slocum asked, leaning now against the far wall. "The life of sin?"

She offered a small, bitter laugh. "Life of sin, song, and so-called drink," she chuckled mirthlessly. "It takes a lot of work to get into hell these days. Just ask any of them girls up there."

"It ain't what you would call upstanding work, now, is it?" Slocum said. She was becoming just a little too self-righteous to suit his taste.

"It ain't upstanding, but it ain't dishonest, neither," she answered harshly. "You remember that. One day they're going to be writing about this part of the country. And mark my words: They ain't going to be writing about the women. They ain't going to be writing about the children, neither."

"Should they?"

She sighed then, and stiffened her back. "I seen whores lend a cowboy enough for a saddle when he didn't have nothing," she said. "I seen women, honest women now, do the work of two men, knowing they would lay back at night and pretend they liked the smell of whiskey and the grunting."

"A lot of men work a lick, too," Slocum said.

Kate was seemingly lost in her own thoughts. "Men," she said. "Men are strange creatures. If someone told me they was from the moon, I'd half believe them. Two years ago, I had this girl, she went and got herself with a child. These two old boys, they come down from the hills. Haven't seen a female in maybe two years. Hardest looking types I ever put my eyes on. I thought they'd as like to bust every bed in the house. Know what they did?"

Slocum shrugged, wanting to let Kate finish.

"Spent two, maybe three, hours playing with that baby," Kate said. "Not playing with it exactly, just staring like. Neither of them had seen a baby for longer than they had a woman. Sat there where I'm sitting now, their eyes big as saucers, staring and making faces. When they finally went and picked out their girls, they did it lickety-split and came back to stare at the baby. I have to tell you, I was half thinking of charging them. They would have paid, too."

Slocum, hearing enough, said, "I'm turning in."

"You sleeping down here tonight, or are you fixing to join me?" Kate asked.

"Is that an invitation?" he countered, half fearing what the answer would be.

"It's whatever you want it to be," she said, then headed off to bed.

Slocum watched her move through the door and then followed Kate to her bed.

It was the next day when the wagon pulled up to the house. Slocum, asleep from the previous night's exertions with Kate, was slow to rise, even with the noise reaching him from the parlor. At first it sounded like a group of men, customers, but then he heard a strange woman's voice joining the commotion and he knew that it was something else.

Pulling himself slowly from bed, he looked out the window and judged it to be sometime after noon, maybe even getting on toward suppertime. If it was late enough, it might be customers. Then again, it might be some people from town sent up on Mac's orders to cause some mischief.

By the time he entered the parlor, he saw that the girls had formed a tight circle around the guests and were chattering hurriedly. Judging from their tone of voice and the giggling that was taking place, he knew he didn't have too much to worry about.

Taking a place at the edge of the small crowd, he saw that the visitors consisted of two men and a woman. The men, one of which was old and the other young, were dressed somewhat like shopkeepers in somber dark coats and low-crowned hats. The woman was another story altogether. She was dressed in a bright purple dress that included enough material to make three ordinary dresses. There was no doubt that she was pretty, but in a way that Slocum judged to be flashy. Were it not for the way she held her head, like a queen or something, Slocum would have guessed her for either a saloon girl who dealt cards and served drinks or an older banker's young wife. Both of which, Slocum knew, had more in common than either one would admit.

"So, there we were, stranded in this wretched little town," the woman said. "Absolutely stranded, when that message arrived by telegraph," the woman said, throwing her hands around as she spoke. "My dear, dear girls, you have no idea—none at all—how grateful we were. No sailor lost at sea could be more grateful than we were at the news the telegraph bore to us."

"It was most fortunate," the older man said, his voice a deep baritone. "Most fortune in timing and substance."

Kate, spotting Slocum, moved away from the crowd to join him. "Actors," she said, nodding back to the small gathering. "Actors for Mac's opera house."

"I was wondering what they were going to put in it," Slocum answered.

"They came in from Carson," she continued. "They thought they were lost when they spotted the place and turned up the trail."

"Mac promised them twenty dollars a week and half of everything the theater earns in the bargain."

"You planning on telling them they ain't got a chance of seeing either one?" Slocum asked, his eyes fastened on the group.

"I thought on it," she answered. "You got feelings about it one way or the other?"

"Always better to have friends than not," Slocum said. "Better feed them, too."

Kate nodded, acknowledging the wisdom of Slocum's suggestion, then headed back to the girls who surrounded the actors. It only took her a short time to lead her guests back into the kitchen, where she and her girls began preparing food for the actors.

Slocum took a seat and introduced himself.

"I should take it, then, sir, that you are the proprietor of this fair and necessary establishment?" the old man asked.

"Hell, he's just a hired hand," Kate called over her shoulder. "I own it."

"Well then, hired hand or not, I should introduce myself and my colleagues," the man said. "This is the beautiful Vivian Parkhurst, he said."

The woman in the purple dress nodded, her eyes fastening on Slocum as she offered him a hint of a gracious smile. Her hair, he saw, from under the purple hat, was a dark reddish brown. Her skin was as white as the inside of a fresh biscuit.

Slocum nodded back and smiled.

"And this, sir," the older gent said, "this is Joseph Huntsford, the finest actor ever to stride the boards, other than myself, of course."

Slocum reached out a hand to the pale youth with blond hair. The young man accepted it across the table with a firmer shake than Slocum expected.

"And I, sir, am Thaddeus Malwroy," the older man continued. "*The* finest actor to speak the words of the great bard as well as lesser-known masters of the craft."

Slocum shook hands with the older gent, then said, "You know anything about Mac?"

"Our new employer?" came the answer. "Why no, sir, only that he is a man of worldly tastes and local influence. Am I not correct in this?"

"He's the world's worst sonofabitch," Kate said.

A few of the girls standing to the side murmured in profound agreement.

"And just how, precisely, do these ungentlemanly traits exhibit themselves?" Vivian asked. It was the way she asked it that Slocum knew that she thought that perhaps Kate was either lying or not accustomed to the more sophisticated tastes of local royalty.

"He's a cheat," Slocum said. "He's a cheat, a liar, and a killer."

"Dear . . ." Vivian said. "A killer, a murderer."

"A cheat, you say?" Malwroy added.

"The worst kind of cheat and the worst kind of killer," Kate offered, bringing a pot of coffee and cups to the table.

"He's the kind that pays others to do his killing for him and the kind of cheat that steals what he don't need from folks who do need it."

"My, that sounds absolutely horrid," Vivian answered.

"It ain't nice," Kate said.

"If I may, perhaps you can enlighten us somewhat, as to how he goes about this?" the young man, Huntsford, said.

And they did. Slocum began the story, but in no time at all Kate jumped in, mostly agreeing with everything Slocum offered and then adding more. After that, the girls got their chance. And when they were through, the trio were slumped back in their seats.

"Well, this is most unexpected," Malwroy sighed. "Most unexpected and unpleasant."

"And you're sure he'll try the same with us?" Huntsford asked.

"I'd bet on it," Slocum answered. "The way I would say it would happen is that he'll use you for as long as people will pay. After that, you'll be lucky to get out of town with the clothes on your back."

"My word," Vivian sighed. "It seems as if we've just gotten ourselves into a mess."

"No fear," Malwroy added. "No fear at all, my dear. This situation reminds me of the time I was employed by the Russian duke. He was a scoundrel and a bounder I would stake against the worst of them. Claimed a love of the bard, but had none at all. But worse, he had no money as well. As an actor and a man of the world, I can forgive almost anything, including an ignorance of the bard. But as an actor and a man of the world, I cannot forgive the other.

Most especially, I cannot forgive it after he misinformed us of his circumstances.''

"What did you do about that?'' Kate asked. "I'd be curious, professionally, seeing as we're in the same kind of business situation.''

The older man and his two friends looked up, bewildered at this comment.

"In the same, I mean we can't exactly take back what we sell,'' Kate explained. "It ain't exactly like taking back a horse or a pig now, is it? Once you sold it, they got it.''

A few of the girls tittered at this.

"Oh, indeed they do my dear lady,'' Malwroy chuckled. "Oh indeed they do.''

"Then what did you do?'' Kate insisted.

"Why, my dear, sweet lady,'' Malwroy began. "My dear lady, we acted. We gave the performance of a lifetime, my colleagues and I. And when we were done, that Russian duke was poorer and wiser.''

15

Slocum and the actors came up with a plan. Slocum had to admit it wasn't much of a plan, but anything was better than loafing around a whorehouse parlor day and night. To do something, anything, was better than taking on the attitude of parlor snake.

They began early the next day. The acting troupe pulled from their wagon a large trunk as well as several small bags. Setting up the tools of their trade in Kate's parlor, they went to work on Slocum with a vengeance.

By the time the actors were through with him, Slocum didn't recognize himself. His head was covered with scraggly gray hair, which hung down over his ears and flopped across his eyes, giving him an appearance something like a sheepdog. The gray hair on his head was matched by a gray mustache that extended up to his ears. He had exchanged his everyday clothing for a black frock coat, vest, and trousers that were so threadbare that he thought if he sat down, the seat of his pants would rip.

"Marvelous, absolutely marvelous," Malwroy exclaimed, stepping back to admire his own handiwork.

"That's the way he's gonna look old?" Kate asked, casting an appraising eye Slocum's way.

"The way he looks old now, anyway," Vivian replied. "But it still looks like him. I mean if you get up close and all."

The old thespian took a step back, squinting. "If they got a good look at you," he said.

"He needs something," Vivian said. "Something *big.*"

The old man hesitated, taking her remark under consideration before reaching a hand into a bag similar to those used by doctors. "Yes, something big," he said, searching the jumbled contents a full minute before pulling from it a small tin. "Something that will distract them, I would think."

Slocum watched as the old man unscrewed the tin and extracted from it a large wart from which a single black, wiry hair grew. "Where are you thinking of putting that?" he asked, a streak of unexpected vanity showing itself.

"Fear not," Thad answered as he applied a small dab of glue to the back end of the wart. "I can assure you, it isn't genuine."

"He's too cheap to buy a genuine one," Vivian said, deadpan.

"Ah, your sense of humor is endearing, my lovely child," Thad said as he leaned in close to Slocum's nose and applied the wart to one side.

Slocum felt the glue harden almost immediately, tightening his skin.

Thad stepped back, once again admiring his own work. "Ah, perfect," he said. "I can assure you that wart has a long and glorious history. It has been worn by some of the most accomplished thespians ever to act on the stage on three continents."

Slocum answered by giving Kate a long look.

She answered by saying, "It ain't exactly what I would call handsome."

"A glass, by all means, please bring the boy a glass," Thad exclaimed, eager for another review of his efforts.

One of the girls who had been standing off to the side ran from the room in search of a mirror. She returned almost immediately holding a small, ornate silver mirror.

Slocum took the mirror and studied himself carefully. Yes, he could see exactly how the wart worked. Even studying himself in the mirror, he could not take his eyes from it. The long hair that protruded from its center extended almost a full inch. It was so gloriously ugly that it drew all attention to it. "It's like a cardsharp," he said at last as he put the mirror down, understanding that it worked the same way as crooked dealers who use one hand to move the cards with a flourish as the other goes about its dirty business.

"Exactly," Thad exclaimed. "Believe me, my good man, they will not see you. They will only see the wart and possibly your nose. If asked to describe you, they will describe the wart in glorious detail."

Slocum rose and walked across the room to the door. "Well, we better get going," he said with a nod.

Thad remained where he stood, a frown spreading on his

lips. "Not like that, we don't," he answered. "Not with you walking like the spry youth you are."

The old man was right, of course. Slocum had simply stood up and walked the way he always did.

"Now, come back and do it again," Thad commanded.

Slocum sat back down and then stood again, this time edging himself up slowly off the chair and walking to the door with a tentative gait.

"No, no, no my dear boy," Thad said. "You're old, not in leave of your senses. Like this!"

Slocum watched as the old man sat down and then rose to walk across the room. He moved in his normal fashion, slightly stooped and somewhat fighting an ache in his bones.

"You do that pretty good," Vivian said. "You should play an old man."

"Enough of your churlishness," Thad answered. "Let the poor boy rehearse."

Slocum took the seat and reenacted Thad's old man walk.

"Perfect, absolutely perfect," Thad said, then handed Slocum a black planter's hat from the open trunk. "Now, put this on and we shall leave for Paradise."

"Aren't you forgetting something?" Vivian asked.

"Joseph, of course," Malwroy answered. "Where is that dear boy?"

"I wonder, too," Vivian said, the sarcasm dripping from her voice.

"I'll fetch him," the girl who had brought the mirror volunteered. "I know where he is, all right."

A short time later, Huntsford came through the door,

fastening his pants together. The girl who fetched him and another of Kate's girls stood behind him.

"No time for that sort of thing now," Malwroy said.

"I wouldn't worry, he doesn't need much time," Vivian added.

"And no time for bickering like children," Malwroy commanded. "We're off to meet our new employer."

Slocum saw the new opera house as they approached town. Completely finished now, it rose above all the other buildings in Paradise. Clearly, it was too large for the town. Judging from its outside, Slocum would guess that it could hold every man, woman, and child in Paradise and still have enough room remaining for a good portion of the livestock as well. But such is the nature of civic pride.

It was midafternoon when the four of them were ushered into Mac's backroom office. If Mac recognized Slocum, he showed no sign of it. Crane, too, as he guided them in, seemed to not recognize Slocum, his eyes fastening on the huge wart and not coming off it until Vivian walked by.

Mac, puffed up behind his desk, did not rise to greet them. Rather, he stared with an appraising eye. "I thought it was three," he said at last, his eyes taking all of them in.

"An associate, a talented actor by any definition," Thad said.

"I won't be paying any extra, talented or no," Mac said. "I asked for three, and I'm paying for three."

"And indeed you won't," Thad answered graciously. "Think of it as a bargain, as it were."

Talk of a bargain seemed to relax Mac a little. He allowed himself to unpuff just slightly. "I suppose you were a little bit curious as to why I asked you to come to Paradise," he began.

"I assumed it was to perform," Thad said. "A good actor is never in doubt as to his popularity. He never questions it"

"Quite right," Mac said, not certain what he was agreeing to. "As you know, we have a new opera house. I want a month's worth of performances."

"And a fine theater it appears," Thad answered. "Really beautiful."

"Damn right it's fine," Mac said. "Built by one of the best architects within a thousand miles."

Thad nodded in acknowledgment. "Now, what would you like us to perform?" he asked. "The great bard perhaps? Or perhaps something a little more modern? A farce?"

"No, no, no, none of that business," Mac said. "None of that."

"Ah then, something to appeal to the more sophisticated tastes," Thad exclaimed. "Excellent! A night of enriching poetry and prose from the masters! Excellent!"

"No! No damn poetry! None," Mac said. "I hired you to play a role. My role, what I say!"

All four of them could only stare.

"Tell me, can you play a preacher?" Mac asked. "A real fire-and-brimstone preacher? Can you make the poor pathetic scum in this town smell hell, really smell it?"

Thad seemed to hesitate at this. "If it was in the play—" he began.

"Damn it! Now, listen to me," Mac roared. "There is

no play. I want you to be a preacher. I want you to get up on that stage and put the fear of hell and damnation into those bastards. Do you understand that?''

''You want me to preach?'' he asked mildly. ''You want me to preach from the Good Book?''

''From my book!'' Mac shot back. ''Damn it, I want you to preach from *my book.*''

Thad, still more than a little confused, asked, ''And the message contained in your book?''

''Hard work and the eradication of sin in all its despicable forms,'' Mac said.

''Like fornication?'' Thad tried tentatively.

''Yes!'' Mac said, a smile breaking out on his face.

''And the vanity of possessions,'' the actor added.

''Yes, yes, exactly right,'' Mac shouted out delightedly.

''Perhaps also the bitter harvest of sloth?'' the actor tried, warming to the idea. ''And the virtues of hard work?''

''Yes, yes, yes!''

Thad, too, began to smile, feeling he now understood his new employer. ''And the twin evils of drink and gambling!''

''No, damnit!'' Mac responded immediately. ''No, nothing about those things, you idiot. I own the saloon! You start people thinking about those things, and you'll put me out of business quick.''

Thad was a little taken aback.

''If I wanted someone to talk about them things, I would have called in a real preacher to do the job. Trouble is, once you get in some real preacher, they're hard to get shut of. Next thing you know, you got women baking pies for 'em and inviting them over to Sunday dinner. Then they start into wanting a church of their own, all sorts of non-sense. Isn't that right, Mr. Crane?''

Crane, standing by the door, answered, ''Yep, you're right there, Mac.''

''Mr. Crane here, he has a hell of a time just keeping them out,'' Mac said. ''Towns like Paradise attract them, like big-eared dogs attract ticks. Now, I'm only confiding in you because, first off, I know you're a man of the world and would understand what I'm talking about.''

''I think I understand perfectly,'' Thad answered.

''The other reason I don't mind telling you is that I know that if any of you, including you missy, start gossiping, then I'll kill you,'' Mac added.

''I think we're all in agreement,'' Thad replied.

''Good, now, drinking, gambling, working on the Sabbath, let 'em do those. Let them love their neighbor for all I give a damn,'' Mac explained. ''Just preach against whoring and not working. Can you do that? Can you preach them things and pass the plate?''

''Pass the plate?'' Thad asked, smelling additional money. ''You mean among the faithful who gather eagerly to hear my sermon?''

''Yes, absolutely,'' Mac said. ''Pass the damned plate. Just remember, all of you, if you touch a dime of it, I'll have Mr. Crane here put a bullet in your brainpan. Isn't that right Mr. Crane?''

''Yes sir,'' Mac's hired gun answered from his post at the door.

16

"Ah, he's a fine piece of work, your Mac is," Thad said when they were out on the street.

"You're not actually thinking of going along with this craziness?" Vivian exclaimed incredulously.

"I'd appreciate your help," Slocum said. "You can see what the ladies and I are up against here."

"Indeed, he's a scoundrel and a rogue of the first order," Thad muttered as he began to walk to where they had hitched the wagon. "A genuine tragedy in the making. But I fear I can't resist it."

"Then you'll do something?" Slocum asked, a little surprised that after actually meeting Mac the old actor would go along with a plan, any plan.

Thad kept walking, apparently deep in thought. Finally he said, "It will be our greatest performance."

"One that will get you killed or all of us killed," Joseph

said. "These men, they aren't fooling."

"And neither am I, neither am I," Thad replied solemnly. "Think of it as a test, the greatest test of your craft and art."

"Dying isn't any kind of test," Joseph shot back. "If that crazy man hears a rumor, a damn whisper that we're up to something, he'll kill us."

"Fear? Is that what I am hearing from you?" Thad asked, coming to a halt in front of the wagon. "Is that what is worrying you, Joseph? Fear?"

"Damn right," the young actor said.

"And I didn't exactly plan on dying any time soon, either," Vivian added. "Thad, this whole thing is just crazy. Let's pack up and keep on until Carson City."

"Listen, if you folks don't want any part of this, I'll understand," Slocum said. "I know it isn't your fight. I can understand that."

"Stage fright is all it is," Thad said. "I've never known an actor worth his wagers that wasn't stricken with it before a performance. It is, I daresay, what drives us to greatness.

"Listen and wait," Thad continued. "I give you this advice in all sincerity. Listen and wait until you hear your parts. Then, after you have heard them, you'll be free to leave."

This bit of talk seemed to shut both of the actors up. A few minutes later, they had stabled their team at the livery and were in the hotel. Crowded into a small room, Thad prepared to tell each the part they would be required to play. Slocum didn't know when or where, but somehow the old codger had concocted a plan.

"I myself will play the preacher," Thad said, bowing his

head. "Admittedly, it is the lead, but remember that each part grows to meet the actor's skill. I will be the man of God, a humble servant, yet filled with biblical fury and vengeance for sinners. Repent you must and repent you will."

"What about me?" Vivian asked, leaning against a wall, her eyes hard and her mouth set.

"Ah, dear girl," Thad said, his voice soft and low. "The role of a lifetime. You are an angel of mercy. Once a soiled dove, you fled your miserable and degrading life in Saint Louis in which your depravity knew no bounds. Two, three, four men in a single day and night—perhaps even more, yes, certainly more—"

"I get the idea," Vivian snapped.

Thad stopped quickly, abandoning the numbers, and said, "Now, once again you are as pure as the driven snow on the highest mountaintop. Your voice and eyes clear. And somehow, more desirable for the transformation. As if somehow you were only a step, a thought, a small slip away from recasting yourself into the life of depravity. Because isn't that what all men want? The innocent with secret dark knowledge of the ways of the world."

A small smile spread out on her lips. Somehow she understood the part completely.

"What about me?" Joseph asked.

Thad looked from Vivian to the young man who was leaning against a dresser. Then, smiling, he said, "Why, a fancy man, of course. A procuror of young women who has seen the error of his ways. A brawler and a killer who is able to cast a snake charmer's magic over women."

When Joseph allowed himself to smile, it was almost a

smirk, but not quite. He was already imagining himself in the role.

"But now, now like dear, sweet, innocent Vivian, you've seen the error of your noxious ways," Thad continued. "You have tossed away your dagger and belly-gun. And you now use that same charm to perform in the service of all that is good. You are the man that mothers want to escort their pure young daughters. A friend and protector of child, woman, and animal alike."

"I see it, yes, I believe I do," Joseph said somewhat dreamily.

"Do you think you're up to the part, boy?" Thad asked, smiling broadly.

"I can play it," Joseph said. "Easily."

"Good then, you'll all do it?" Thad asked.

Before they could answer, Slocum asked, "What part for me? I'll be in this thing, too, right?"

Thad cast an appraising eye on Slocum, then answered, "You're the halfwit that passes the plate."

Slocum nodded and despite himself felt somewhat uneasy about the role he was chosen to play.

"I'm assuming, of course, that you know how to apply those firearms if the need should somehow arise."

Slocum nodded.

"Fine, fine then," Thad said. "When I preach, you pass the plate from front to back. When you reach the back of the theater, I want you to stand there and keep the rabble in line."

"Now that you're mentioning guns and all, I was just wondering if you had any ideas about the play?" Vivian asked. "I mean beyond the roles."

"Indeed I do," Thad answered. "It came to me in a flash as we were conversing with that madman. To quote the bard's finest creation, *Hamlet,* 'The play's the thing.' "

"What thing is that?" Slocum asked. "Exactly what thing?"

"Listen now, my friends, and I'll reveal it," Thad said. "But don't talk until I've finished, then we can rewrite as we all see fit."

Thad spoke for nearly half an hour. And during the entire time, Slocum stood nearly motionless. The plan seemed to be thought out to its finest detail. Just from listening to the plan, it seemed like it would work. The only problem Slocum could see was that everyone on all sides of the thing had to do exactly as Thad said they would.

"It seems to me you're cutting it kind of close," Slocum finally said.

"I was about to say the same thing," Vivian added. "We know our parts, but what if they miss their lines, as it were?"

"Then we improvise," Thad answered quickly. "Which reminds me of a story I'd like to share with you."

It was well after midnight when Slocum finally left the room. As he made his way out of town on foot, he told himself that he didn't want to spend another night in the hotel, but in truth, he wanted to see Kate.

On his way back to the whorehouse, he walked slowly, avoiding the road and keeping ten or fifteen yards into the trees. When he finally arrived, he saw the lights in the parlor burning brightly, casting a yellowish glow over the front porch.

When he knocked on the door, one of the girls answered, her face lit by a smile which quickly faded when she saw who the gentleman caller was. "Kate's in the back," the girl said, leading Slocum into the parlor.

Inside there were a couple of ranch hands keeping company with two other girls. The boys were probably just arriving or just leaving.

Slocum nodded to the ranch hands and they nodded back. Then he made his way through the kitchen to the back of the house. Kate was standing just beyond the stairs, her eyes fixed on some distant point in the darkened treeline.

"You had many customers tonight?" he asked.

"There been some customers, but I ain't had any of them," Kate answered, turning to Slocum.

He smiled at the joke, then stepped down into the yard to stand next to her, letting his eyes follow her gaze into the trees.

Turning her eyes then, as if she didn't want him to see the spot she studied, Kate said, "Damn, but you're one ugly sonofabitch."

He recoiled slightly at the insult, then remembered the makeup. "I'm just an old man looking for some womanly comfort," he said.

"Is that why you came back?" she asked, her voice serious as she fixed him with her gaze.

"That, and to tell you Thad has a plan," Slocum answered. "You didn't think I'd come back?"

"It crossed my mind," she said. "Maybe it's the business I'm in. It doesn't take long until you learn not to expect too much."

"Then I'll try not to let you down," Slocum said, leading her back through the house toward her room.

As they passed the parlor, one of the girls muttered, "And she's the one always talking about not ever giving any of it away."

"I heard that!" Kate yelled from behind the closed door and was rewarded by a muffled round of giggles from the parlor.

Almost before the words were out of her mouth, Slocum took Kate in his arms and kissed her hard on her full, red lips. Then, reaching up, he pulled the pins from her hair, letting it fall freely down over her shoulders. When it was all the way let out, he buried his face in it, smelling the scent of harsh soap, perfume, and Kate's own womanly scent.

She responded by pushing her face against his hard chest, then reaching her lips up to kiss the flesh of his neck just above his collar.

In no time at all, Slocum managed to slip out of the borrowed clothes as he watched Kate undress with similar haste. When they were done, they embraced again, his already erect member rubbing against the smooth flesh of her belly.

Reaching down with one hand, she began to stroke his manhood, letting the sensitive underside slide back and forth along the smooth skin of her palm.

Then he lowered his hand and brought his fingers up slightly to graze against her silken thatch. At his first touch, he felt her wetness. It seemed to drip off her hair. Exploring further, he felt the soft, pouting lips beyond the thatch. He nuzzled a thumb gently between the lips, feeling more wetness. A low moan escaped from her mouth and she quivered.

"Oh, John Slocum," she sighed, turning softer in his arms as she continued to stroke him. "You are one of a kind. The rarest kind."

Slocum took a small, tenative step toward the bed; as if in a dance, she followed without letting go of his manhood.

When they eased themselves down on the soft bed, Slocum once again let his fingers play along her tuft and the moist prize beyond. Very slowly he let a finger edge between the two pouting lips to feel the hard little nub. At his first touch of the sensitive nub, she moaned again and drew herself close to him.

Easing his head down, he began to suck on one of her nipples, feeling it grow hard and erect in his mouth.

"Now, please," she whispered. "I'm ready. Please."

Slowly he let the nipple slide from his mouth and withdrew his finger, then brought himself up on his knees between her widely spread legs.

Reaching down, she grabbed his member again and slowly guided it into her. With the first touch of his hard shaft between her lips, she let out a small cry, then arched her back upward to take him completely inside her.

They lay like that for a long time without moving. Then, slowly, Slocum pulled back, letting the long shaft slide moist and glistening from within her.

When all but the tip was removed, he paused for a moment, then slowly, teasingly, eased back inside her.

Little by little, he moved faster, until he was drawing his shaft in and out at a steady pace. And with each movement of his shaft, she moved, matching his pace and extracting as much pleasure as he did.

Looking down, Slocum studied her face. Her eyes were closed and her mouth gaped half open. Even in such a pose, she was beautiful. No, it was in such an attitude that she was most beautiful, he thought.

Feeling like a thief, studying her face with her eyes closed, he ducked his head and took one of her bouncing nipples again into his mouth. Biting it gently, he drew a groan of pleasure from her lips as her arms encircled him and her feet came up behind him so that her ankles joined at the small of his back.

She pulled him in with her strong, shapely legs and urged him to move faster.

As he felt himself reaching climax, he let the nipple fall from his mouth and grabbed both breasts with his hands, feeling their soft fullness.

Suddenly she let out a long, low cry, and he felt her squeeze his member from inside. Just as the cry was dying on her lips, he exploded inside her in wave after wave of pleasure.

Later, entwined in each other's arms, she looked up at him. Her eyes were full and bright. There was a strangely earnest look on her face. "John Slocum, I do believe you are the finest kind," she whispered, then let herself settle in against his chest.

17

Slocum found Thad, Vivian, and Joseph in the dining room of the hotel. To call it an actual dining room might have been an exaggeration, but that was what the clerk called the three tables set in an oversized alcove at the far end of the hotel.

It wasn't the dining room that held Slocum's attention, however; it was the actors' dress. Somehow, during the night, Thad and his compatriots had transformed themselves in both dress and manner into the roles they were set to play. Then he remembered that he was still wearing the makeup and clothing from the day before.

Slocum studied them for a moment as they hunched over a newspaper, then walked across the lobby to the smaller table.

"Excellent. We thought that a replacement might be necessary," Thad said, looking up from the paper. "Or worse, we feared that we might be forced to close the show.''

''He's just been tomcatting around,'' Vivian said. ''My guess is he snuck himself out to visit Kate last night.''

''Inconsequential,'' Thad said, hurriedly. ''My dear boy, just take a look at this.''

Slocum took the paper and began reading the page Thad pointed toward. Most of the page was taken up by a long editorial bearing Thad's name as a preacher. The editorial seemed to go on for some time talking about sin, though never really mentioning it. Then, somewhere toward the end, whoring was mentioned specifically. Somebody reading the story would think that whoring was not only the worst possible sin, but the only one that existed.

''That's quite a piece of writing,'' Slocum said. ''You work fast, don't you?''

''Not I,'' Thad answered, pulling back a little. ''You have the good Mr. Mac to thank. By all indications, this little sermon has been ready for days, perhaps weeks. He was awaiting only our arrival.''

''Came by early this morning, said he had a newspaperman in Seattle write it up,'' said Vivian.

''Tell him the rest of it,'' Joseph put in.

''Yes, quite right,'' Thad said. ''It appears that Mac, upholder of civic virtue, is so delighted with our initial meeting that he feels there might be steady work in it for us.''

Slocum, who had been leaning over the group, pulled a chair from the other table and sat down. ''You mean like settling down in Paradise. Playing preacher forever?''

''No, far too dangerous,'' Thad said. ''What he proposed was that we come through, perhaps every four months or so, to preach.''

"Preach what, exactly? I mean, after he figures Kate's out of the whore business?"

"The best part, my dear lad," Thad said. "Preach against sloth and promote the virtues of hard work, for one thing. Preach the message of earthly rewards bestowed on the worthy and the hardworking. Preach—"

"Any damned thing he says," Vivian interrupted. "If he bought too much flour for the general merchandise, he'd want Thad to preach the virtue of pies. It would go like that, understand?"

"I got a pretty good idea," Slocum answered. "I knew he was low, but I didn't know how low."

"Well, now you know," Joseph said.

It was just then that the clerk arrived with the food. He carried it on a large tray, clanking heavily with plates. For an instant it seemed as if the tray, plates, coffeepot, and all, would topple, but he regained his balance and managed to set the food down without too much trouble.

"I didn't know they had a kitchen," Slocum said.

"They don't," Thad answered. "The good lad runs across to the saloon for the food."

"Why not just go over there?"

"A man of my stature, in a common saloon?" Thad asked, feigning outrage.

The four of them began to chuckle over the slight joke. But it was the nervous laughter of uneasiness. However, before it ended, a voice said, "You folks enjoying yourselves?"

Slocum looked up, turning his head upward and toward the door. There, standing over him, was Crane.

"My good man, indeed we are," Thad answered. "And

do extend our most heartfelt appreciation to Mac for his warm welcome and hospitality.''

"I don't much care for actors and that kind of trash,'' Crane said, talking to Thad, but looking straight at Slocum.

"Maybe they don't care for you all that much, either,'' Vivian snapped back.

"They're strange,'' Crane said. "They got themselves strange ways. I don't much care for that.''

"Perhaps you've never fully understood the art form,'' Thad tried. "What sir, is your favorite play?''

"I don't know no plays,'' Crane said, still studying Slocum. "I don't care much for made-up words and that kind of thing. It's all made up, it ain't nothing.''

Thad, noting Crane's interest in Slocum, rose quickly from his seat. "Sir, perhaps a bit of the bard will ignite the poet in you,'' he said. Then, without waiting for a reply, he began, "Ay, every inch a king: When I do stare, see how the subject quakes. I pardon that man's life. What was thy cause? Adultery? Thou shalt not die: die for adultery! No: The wren goes to't, and the small gilded fly does lecher in my sight. Let copulation thrive—''

"What in hell was that?'' Crane asked, now studying Thad as if the older man was mad.

"*Lear,* my dear sir, *King Lear,* one of the great bard's finest. Act four, scene six, if my memory serves.''

Crane paused then, thinking. "I know Mr. Mac don't want no more talk about some king watching flies humping and like that,'' he said at last. "You get up and start talking about that sort of thing, I know he ain't gonna be happy.''

"Indeed,'' Thad answered, nodding.

"He ain't gonna be happy at all,'' Crane said. "That's

something I can promise you.''

''I was merely demonstrating the beauty of—''

''Don't demonstrate nothing for me,'' Crane said. ''Demonstrate your old ass up on that stage and scare them ol' boys out of whoring. Leastways until Mac can build himself his own whorehouse.''

''Yes sir,'' Joseph said. ''We'll scare them stupid.''

''They already are stupid,'' Crane said, preparing to leave. ''If they weren't stupid, they wouldn't listen to the likes of you.''

''Have every confidence,'' Thad said.

Crane gave him a hard look, then turned to the door.

''Charming young man,'' Thad said when Crane was out of earshot.

''He knows,'' Slocum replied. ''He knows who I am. That sonofabitch recognized me.''

''Nonsense,'' Thad answered quickly. ''He thinks he knows something, but he isn't sure what it is.''

''He's right, Thad,'' Vivian said. ''He's gonna recognize him sooner or later.''

''And the minute he does, all of us, we're as good as dead,'' Joseph said.

Thad looked to Slocum for some piece of advice.

''The boy's right,'' Slocum said. ''Once he figures out who I am, he won't waste time.''

''You have any ideas regarding this new turn of events?'' Thad asked. ''A useful piece of improvisation, perhaps?''

Slocum paused, thinking, then said, ''There's something I can do, but I'll have to change back into my clothes.''

A half hour later, Slocum, feeling a little strange dressed as himself, walked down the street. It was funny, he thought, how just changing his clothing could make him feel completely different. Suddenly, he didn't feel as safe as he had dressed as one of Thad's actors.

It was early morning and the street was crowded with ranchers and miners doing their errands in town. A couple of Mac's boys were busy putting up posters announcing that a famous preacher had arrived in town and would be holding the first of several meetings in a week's time.

When he reached the saloon, he noticed that Crane and three of his men were loafing on the boards. At the first sight of Slocum, one of the men nudged Crane.

"Well, you got guts, I'll give you that," Crane said. "Showing up here and all."

Crane almost looked pleased to see Slocum. For his part, the big Southerner just smiled.

"You ain't got nothing to say for yourself?" Crane asked.

Slocum shrugged. He wanted to speak as little as possible, fearful that Crane would recognize him by voice.

"Well you just ain't too bright," Crane continued. "After what you did to them boys. I ain't found them, but I will. And when I do, they're gonna hang you. Do it on a Saturday morning. Make a picnic of it for the folks."

The men standing around Crane laughed at the feeble joke. They laughed in the way that all half-witted men laugh when their boss tries to tell a joke. And Crane accepted it, the way all weak men in a position of authority accept the hollow laughter of those who surround them.

Slocum, meeting Crane's suddenly hard gaze, stepped up on the boards. For an instant, it looked as if Slocum intended to walk over Crane, but then he turned slightly and pushed through the doors into the saloon.

Inside was the cool morning darkness of saloons everywhere. The place was nearly empty, save for a few hardy morning drinkers. There were not nearly as many men inside as Slocum would have liked, but he would think of something.

When he bellied up to the bar, the bartender was slow in coming, as if he were about to perform a task that he knew would lead to his own demise. "I don't want no trouble," he said, as he approached Slocum. "None at all, you understand?"

"I'm just here for a drink, friend," Slocum answered and pulled a coin from his pocket. "Whiskey, if it isn't too much trouble."

The bartender didn't answer but turned to the bottles behind him filled with amber-colored liquor and pulled down the nearest one. When he had the small glass topped off, he took Slocum's coin and strode away.

"I thought you would have taken them whores' money and just left," came Crane's voice from behind Slocum. "It's a low thing to do, stealing from a whore, but it would have been the smartest thing you ever did."

Slocum could feel the cold hate creeping over him, tightening the muscles in his back and neck. It felt good, like an old friend. But still, he did not answer.

"I figured you would have had your fill and bedded all of them and rode out," Crane continued. "Maybe stole something like a chicken on the way."

A few of Crane's men guffawed from their positions at the door to show their apparent appreciation of their superior's obvious wit.

"Whiskey!" Crane yelled down the bar, now standing next to Slocum.

The bartender came walking back, a worried look on his face. "I don't want no trouble, Mr. Crane," he said. "Please, not in the bar."

"There ain't gonna be no trouble," Crane answered with a bitter smile. "I just figured on joining my friend here in a little drink."

The bartender poured the whiskey and vanished. Slocum noticed that he did not take up a position at the far end, but rather kept walking, straight toward the exit at the back. Slocum knew he would have to work fast.

"You Dixie sumbitch, ain't you got nothing to say?" Crane said, taking up his drink slowly.

Slocum turned to him and stared for a long time. Then he said in a harsh whisper, "I'm gonna kill you, you know that? I'm gonna kill you and you're gonna die like a damned dog."

"You think so, do you?" Crane answered in a loud voice, so his men could hear. "You think you're gonna kill me, do you? Well, you're a dead man. I'd just as leave shoot you in the back as look at you. Track you to Carson, San Francisco, anywhere."

"That's the difference between you and me," Slocum said, still speaking in a whisper. "I'm gonna do it in a fair fight. And I'm gonna do it here. Right now."

The color drained from Crane's face at this. He drained the glass and set it back on the bar. "Right now, you say?"

"Right now, you bastard, unless you ain't got the guts to face me in front of your men in a fair fight," Slocum answered, now speaking loud enough for the men to hear.

"Right now?" Crane asked, his hands flat on the bar.

"Unless you don't have the nerve," Slocum said. "Unless you're afraid. Or maybe it's Mac. You afraid to fight a man without Mac's say-so?"

"I ain't afraid of nobody," Crane said.

"What else does he have you doing," Slocum said, whispering again. "Cleaning out the stalls? Maybe he's gonna breed you to one of his hogs, is that one of your jobs?"

"You bastard," Crane said, nearly yelling as he came off the bar.

"You go out there and rut with them hogs in the slop at night?" Slocum said.

"I'll kill you, you sonofabitch," Crane shouted, as he stepped toward Slocum.

Before Crane's foot came down on the first step, Mac was at the door, yelling, "Crane! Stop it, that's an order!"

Crane swung his head around to take in Mac, standing in the doorway, his bulk nearly filling it. "You stay out of this, you fat sonofabitch!" he yelled, then swung on Slocum.

Slocum ducked his head back, then brought his left hand up to counter the blow. The fist missed Slocum by a good six inches, sending Crane off balance. Slocum swung again and connected hard into the man's gut.

"Stop it instantly!" Mac yelled, as Crane doubled up and rushed forward.

Slocum swung again, bringing his fist up hard into Crane's face. As the blow connected, he could feel the crush of cartilage and flesh as Crane's nose collapsed under the impact.

Despite the pain, Crane kept coming, pushing hard at Slocum as his boots struggled for purchase on the slippery sawdust on the saloon floor. Bringing his knee up hard, Slocum connected again, this time snapping Crane's head back on his neck.

"Stop it immediately!" Mac ordered, his voice thundering through the saloon.

Crane wrapped his arms around Slocum and pushed, sending both of them against the bar. Slocum bent over, and in a voice only Crane could hear, said, "This is it, you bastard. You'll wish you were out back, up behind one of Mac's hogs when I get done with you."

The words sent Crane into a rage. He disengaged himself from Slocum and stood up, presenting his ruined face to the crowd that had now gathered at the windows and door.

"I don't want no trouble," Slocum said, holding his hands up. "This is a crazy man."

Hearing the duplicity, Crane swung blindly and charged again.

Slocum easily stepped away, letting the man crash into the bar.

The blow seemed to knock the breath out of him, doubling him over again as Slocum moved into the center of the saloon.

Gasping for air, Crane came up again, unsteady on shaking legs and filled with incoherent rage.

"Let it go, Crane," Mac ordered. "You've had enough."

"I ain't had nothing," Crane shouted back to his boss.

"He beat you, fair," Mac said. "Now let it be."

"He didn't beat me," Crane insisted, despite all evidence. ''He didn't beat nothing.''

''You do what I say,'' Mac shouted, his face red. ''That's what you're paid for, to do as I say, and I say stop it.''

''Do as he tells you,'' Slocum added. ''Just do as he tells you.''

''He didn't beat me and nobody tells me what to do,'' Crane insisted, his head turning from Mac to Slocum.

''I do, I tell you what to do,'' Mac raged. ''And I'm telling you to let off of this.''

When Crane turned again from Mac to Slocum, the big Southerner made just the faintest sound in his throat that sounded like he was clearing it to everyone but Crane, who knew that it was the sound of a hog.

''You hear me, boy?'' Mac yelled. ''You do whatever I say!''

''You do whatever he says,'' Slocum added. ''Listen to the man who pays you.''

Crane swung on his feet then, bringing his gun hand down and drawing. At first Slocum thought he was drawing on him, then knew that Crane was drawing down on Mac. Crane was fast, but Slocum was faster. Before the gunman could get his pistol half up to his chest to fire, Slocum was already squeezing down on the trigger.

Three shots rang out, blasting the silence from the saloon. The first hit Crane in the jaw, sending a spray of blood and bone across the bar's mirror and sending the gunman spinning. The second shot hit Crane in the neck, snapping his head back at an unnatural angle as the bullet smashed out of the base of his skull on the opposite side. And the third took off the top of his head, sending a large clump of hair and skull sailing through the air to land thudding among the bottles of whiskey.

For a brief, silent moment, Crane remained on his feet, gun still outstretched toward Mac. And then he fell, traveling to the floor like a drowning man sinking into the depths, his gun hand raised above his head, fingers limp around the handle and trigger.

18

"I've got to hand it to you son, you don't take any half measures," Thad said. "None at all."

He was, of course, talking about Slocum having shot Crane. And if he had to be honest, the whole deal hadn't gone the way Slocum had planned. "That wasn't exactly what I had in mind," Slocum said.

"And what was it you had in mind?" Thad asked, pacing his small hotel room, nearly lost in thought. "They say you shot him three times in the head, while he was on the move. Exactly which of those three bullets didn't you intend to hit Crane with?"

"None of them," Slocum said. "I went in there figuring on maybe fighting him, giving him something more to worry about than us."

Thad sat down on his bed and sighed. "And as it turns out, we have something more to worry about," he said. "I don't know if I'm madder at you for nearly ruining my plan, superb as it was, or upstaging me.''

"I can say I'm sorry for your plan," Slocum answered, leaning back against the door. "I'm sorry I went and ruined it like I did. But I ain't sorry I shot that bastard. Not at all.''

"There's an adage in the theater," Thad said, speaking to the floor. "Never perform on the same stage as a child or an animals. They say this because no matter how minor their talent, it is always the child or animal that will reap the applause. Now, I am sorry to say, I can add to the list, a gunfighter.''

"I'm no gunfighter," Slocum answered quickly.

"Then you gave a fine performance of one in that saloon,'' Thad replied, looking up. "The entire town can speak of nothing else.''

"Where's Vivian and Joseph?" Slocum asked, trying to change the subject.

"On stage, as it were," Thad answered. "Trying to snatch a victory from the jaws of defeat into which you so senselessly thrust us.''

"You mean she's going through with it?" Slocum asked.

"Yes, and I must say that your little performance didn't help matters any.''

"And Joseph, too?"

"Yes, yes, we're all going ahead with it," Thad said. "The show, as they say, must go on.''

Slocum knew that Vivian's part called for her to try to seduce Crane. But failing that, she would have to have a go at Mac.

"Listen, I figured to keep myself hidden until tonight," Slocum said.

Thad looked up from his place on the bed and said, "Go then. But be back to the theater on time and in costume."

Slocum made his way out of the hotel and onto the street, just in time to see Mac escorting Vivian and Joseph down the boards. For all the world, they looked like they were part of a preacher's show.

Mac was smiling down on Vivian and engaged in animated conversation, while Joseph walked a few paces behind.

"Ah, my good man, my good man!" Mac called to Slocum when he spotted him.

Slocum's first thoughts were to go for his gun or his horse. But Mac was fast for a fat man. He disengaged himself from Vivian and hurried up to the big Southerner. "A word, if you will, please," he said, his face still holding a smile.

Slocum nodded and let Mac come to him.

"Ah now, I haven't seen you since that unfortunate incident this morning," Mac said. "I have a piece of business to discuss. A little bit of business I think you will find most agreeable."

Slocum nodded again, aware now that Mac intended to settle some debt for saving his life.

"Walk for a moment," Mac said, leading Slocum away from in front of the general merchandise and its loafers.

The two began walking down the boards slowly, Mac so close Slocum could smell the cigar and beer scent mixing with the ladylike perfume he wore. "I'm listening," Slocum said.

"As you know, there is now a position open in my organization," Mac said. "To my way of thinking, you are a natural choice."

"I'm no hired gun," Slocum answered.

Mac let out a small chuckle. "Please, don't think of it in that way," he said. "Think of the position as that of bank manager."

"Bank manager?" Slocum nearly laughed.

"Yes, you would not have to draw a gun, I can assure you of that," Mac said. "Mr. Crane seemed to have a proclivity for it. Though, sadly, his proficiency was not what it might have been."

"Your Mr. Crane talked too much," Slocum answered.

"Yes, indeed, he talked too much, drank too much, and worst of all, he was a bully," Mac said. "Perhaps he was necessary when we were first starting out, but as you can see now, we are a real town. And I require a man of some discrimination. A man of tact. A man of high ideals and a low tolerance for the more unsavory elements."

"A bank manager," Slocum added.

"Exactly!" Mac said. "Just as a bank manager you will be entrusted with the well-being and judicious care of the resources of this noble little hamlet, those being the people. And, like a bank manager, you'd be expected to perform your job in a manner befitting your position. That is, by proxy, delegation, as it were."

"You mean, I wouldn't need to shoot anyone?" Slocum asked bluntly.

"Exactly!" Mac answered delightedly. "Shoot, menace, run off, there are, I daresay, myriad responsibilities. And you, my dear sir, would perform them by proxy, delegating the daily chores to a group of hand-picked men.''

"So, I wouldn't need to get my hands dirty?''

"Sir, when was the last time you happened on a bank manager soiling his own hands with the handling of currency?'' Mac asked, dropping his voice to a confidential whisper. "You would need only manage the men as you see fit. Either by inspiring trust and loyalty in yourself, or distrust and disloyalty among each other, or a combination of the two.''

They were in front of the theater now, and Mac stopped. Hooking his thumbs in the tops of his trousers and pushing out his belly in Slocum's direction, he said, "What say you then?''

Slocum sighed and looked around. "I say, I'm afraid I can't take the offer. But thank you just the same.''

"But you haven't heard the pay yet,'' Mac replied, unpuffing quite a bit.

"Don't need to,'' Slocum said.

"It's a foolish man who turns down work, or accepts work for that matter, without knowing the wages,'' Mac said, leaning in close.

"Not if he doesn't want the work,'' Slocum said, turning slightly to look at the poster that was tacked to the theater door. The poster was an advertisement for Thad's bogus prayer meeting.

Mac, entirely unpuffed now, said, "In that case, sir, I am prepared to offer you one thousand dollars.''

"For what?'' Slocum asked, turning back toward Mac.

"For leaving,'' Mac said. "For saving my life. For both those things. In all due respect, if you are not receiving my money, then I would prefer not to have you linger in town."

"That's the way it has to be?"

"I'm sorry to say, yes," Mac answered. "I would assume that a thousand dollars in gold would clear your accounts with our mutual friend, Kate?"

"Just about," Slocum said.

At this news, Mac let out a small chuckle. "Stop by my office then in the morning and I'll settle our account. After that, I trust you'll be making your way to Carson City shortly thereafter."

"If you're still in town, I'll be there," Slocum said.

Mac seemed to find that funny and began chuckling again. "Well, two in one day was more than I had hoped for," he said. "At the end of today I consider myself lucky just the same."

"Two?" Slocum asked, partially knowing what Mac would say.

"Indeed! You no doubt noticed the young lady in whose company you found me," Mac said.

"Yes, of course."

"Well, sir," Mac said, puffing up a bit. "She is an actor engaged in the production to take place here tonight. I'm telling you this because I do not fear your loyalty, not with a thousand dollars due. In any event, she has secured the rights to open a bawdy house here in town. That is, after your current employer is long gone."

"Who is she?"

"Ha! Perhaps the best piece of it," Mac laughed. "She, sir, is an actress who plays a soiled dove rescued from sin, when in fact, she is far from rescued. You could indeed say she is a soiled dove playing an actress. And she is soon to be my partner in this little enterprise.''

"Sounds complicated," Slocum answered.

"Business is not an easy thing," Mac said. "In fact, it takes a tremendous amount of brainpower to make oneself a success."

Slocum merely shrugged.

"Good-bye to you, then," Mac said suddenly. "And I'll count on seeing you tomorrow morning."

"Bet on it," Slocum answered.

A few hours later, Slocum, Thad, Vivian, and Joseph were standing on the stage of the theater. It was as fine a stage and theater as any Slocum had ever seen. There must have been a hundred, maybe a hundred and twenty-five seats, stretched out before him. A half-dozen chandeliers twice as large as poker tables hung from the ceiling, and the walls were painted pure white. The stage, too, was something to look at. It had a thick red curtain with gold trim out in front and another black curtain at the back. A row of lamps lined the lip of the stage.

Slocum found it hard to believe that the theater didn't exist until a week ago. To build it must have taken every available man in Paradise. But now it was done, and it was by far the best theater Slocum had ever seen in such a small town.

"So, dear Vivian, was your performance successful?" Thad asked as he approached Vivian across the stage.

"Of course," she answered, off-handedly. "He not only wants to go to bed with me, but to go into business with me."

"Excellent," Thad said. "And you, Joseph, what have you learned?"

"Spent most of the day in the barbershop and bath, listening to the loafers," he said. "Seems Mac's hired himself a photographer. Plans to send a picture back East to his bosses and for engraving in the newspapers."

"Ha! Better and better," Thad laughed. "Position this dear man well, then. And by all means, see to it that Mac does get his picture sent back East."

"You still haven't given us our cues," Vivian said.

"Quite right," Thad said. "I have here my sermon, a masterful bit of work, if I do say so myself."

"And?" Joseph asked.

Thad spread the ample pages out on the floor. "I start speaking here," he said, then began pointing at specific places in the text. "Joseph, I introduce you here. And Vivian, you here. You both speak, until here."

"And we leave here?" Vivian asked, pointing now, also.

"Yes, indeed," Thad said. "And our good friend Slocum begins passing the plate while I begin again. By that time, you should be in position."

"And I start, when?" Joseph asked.

"I want you to arrange your cue with Viv," Thad said. "I don't care what it is you say, Viv, just be sure that our dear Joseph can hear you. Remember, there are no rehearsals for this part of our little show."

"Oh, he'll hear me all right," Viv answered. "He better hear me, because I am not doing the encore that fat bastard expects."

"That's it?" Slocum asked. "I just pass the plate?"

"Until Mac's men start toward the stage," Thad said.

"After that, I'm sure you'll be quite busy."

"I heard he has six men left," Joseph said. "And they're all taking orders right from Mac for now."

"Can you handle it?" Thad asked, turning back to Slocum.

"I can handle it," Slocum answered.

19

Slocum, wearing his costume, watched Mac from the back of the theater. Every chair in the large room was filled. He could see miners and ranchers, hardworking people, who maybe came to town four times a year, sitting as obediently as schoolchildren. Two long lines of men stood against either wall, waiting patiently for the show to begin.

Mac stood behind a podium at the center of the stage. He stood there motionless, waiting for the last bit of talking and movement to die down. When he was at last satisfied with the near silence, he cleared his throat loudly, signaling that the show was about to begin.

"Friends, citizens of Paradise," he intoned seriously. "You all know me. You know me as a friend. As an employer. And most of all, I would hope, you know me as a firm but fair man."

There was a scattering of applause at this. Slocum

guessed that it was begun by what was left of Crane's men.

"Some of you have known me for years," Mac continued. "Others among you I have met but recently. Perhaps you know me as a man of some means, of wealth."

With the mention of money, his money, the crowd seemed to draw in its breath, as if they were waiting to see whose house he was about to foreclose on.

"But until very recently, I was a poor man," Mac said. "Perhaps not poor in gold, in money, but in spirit. This bothered me. For if the good Lord loved me enough to make me rich and powerful, if he favored me like that, then why was I poor in spirit? Why did I have that feeling?"

Not a single person in the crowd stirred. Not an eye blinked.

"The answer came to me on one of my frequent trips to San Francisco," Mac said. "There I met a man who could answer my questions. He filled that hole I felt in my soul with wise counsel. Indeed, he has been the confidant of kings and European royalty. He showed me the way not only to a greater love of my fellow man, but, and I say this in all honesty, to greater profits of my far-flung investments."

A small murmur went up through the crowd.

"I say this now, knowing what I now know," Mac continued. "If you are poor, it is your own fault. If you are plagued by disease, it is your own fault. If you are tired, unhappy, confused, sick in mind and spirit, it is your own fault."

At these absurd words, Slocum noticed that the crowd seemed to sink back into their seats, ashamed.

"I say this with all love for my fellow man," Mac roared

and pounded the podium. "If you are not happy with your lot in life, then too damned bad!"

It was as if the crowd had been slammed back at these words. A terrible silence seemed to fill the room, and Mac remained completely still at the podium.

"I say, too damned bad!" Mac repeated. "But I will help you. I will help my community as I have always helped it. At great expense I have brought this same man here, to Paradise. I have brought him here to share his wisdom and knowledge with you!"

The audience, shocked out of its shame, erupted in a roar as Mac gestured to the side of the stage with one extended arm.

The applause seemed to increase as Thad, looking for all the world like a preacher, came out on the stage. He stopped at the side of the podium, then shook hands with Mac. A moment later, Mac was leaving the stage.

"Friends, friends, friends," Thad said, motioning with his hands for the crowd to quiet down. "I come here tonight to tell you of a disease that is spreading in your midst."

Once again, the crowd grew silent.

"This disease, my dear friends, is fornication," Thad said. "When I heard of this town, this town of Paradise, I wanted to come. I needed to come. I practically begged to come. Then I heard of the existence of a den of sin, a pit of hell, a bawdy house. Yes, sir, a bawdy house here in Paradise. Oh, what cruel ironic joke of the wicked to place such a disgrace in a town so aptly named. I had to come because I heard that fornication was taking place there."

Slocum began moving forward now, working his way

toward the side doors that led backstage.

"Yes, I know some of this talk will shock the ladies in the audience," Thad said in a loud, clear voice. "It is usually not a subject for audiences with women. But it is necessary that woman hear it."

As Slocum made his way backstage, he saw Joseph standing by the ropes that held the curtains. The young man, spotting Slocum, tilted his head against the back wall to where the rear curtains hung.

Slocum walked softly toward those back curtains. And there, below the address Thad was giving, he heard Mac's voice speaking in low, confidential terms. "The fools, the ignorant fools," Mac said. "To listen to such drivel and believe it."

Then Slocum heard Viv's voice. "Some people will believe anything."

Peering around the curtains, he saw Mac seated on a stool watching the audience through a small peephole. He had a lewd grin on his face.

"The filthy half-wits," Mac said.

It was then Slocum noticed that Mac seemed sexually excited by what he witnessed through the peephole. The fat man was actually rubbing himself between his massive thighs.

"Come here," he ordered Viv, wrapping an arm around her waist and pulling her close. "Look at those fools."

Thad's voice grew louder and louder. As Thad's speech reached its peak, Mac seemed to grow more excited. His hand was working along the material of his trousers at a frantic pace.

Slocum knew that if he kept up, the plan wouldn't work.

Rushing back to Joseph, he apprised him of the situation.

"Thad's gonna be madder than hell," Joseph said. "He don't like nobody cutting in on his lines."

"Well, there won't be no finish if we don't," Slocum answered. "I'll go try to get a message to Viv."

Joseph nodded as Slocum moved back to the space beside the curtain.

Mac was so totally enraptured by what he saw through the small hole, he didn't notice Slocum signaling to Viv, who had a worried and pleading look on her face.

Nearly running now, Slocum went back to Joseph. "When I give you the signal from the back, drop it," he said. "Viv can't hold out any longer."

"If Thad asks, and he will, I'm blaming you," Joseph said.

"Then blame me," Slocum spat back. "Where's that shotgun?"

Joseph reached down and grabbed the gun from where it rested against the wall.

Shotgun in hand, Slocum now ran the dozen steps back to the curtain. Holding up five fingers, he began to count them down to Viv.

By the time he reached the third finger, Viv said to Mac, "Mac, honey, why don't you take that big fella out and let me go to work on it?"

Mac looked up at her, leering as he unfastened his pants and grabbed his small, erect member.

Slocum counted to one as Mac began to stroke his own organ furiously.

And then Slocum dropped his arm, giving Joseph the signal. There was the *whoosh* of fabric as the back curtain collapsed in a black heap, leaving Mac on the high stool with his organ in hand at center stage.

The crowd let out a collective gasp as Slocum watched Viv run to the opposite end of the stage, just narrowly avoiding being caught in the falling material.

Suddenly there was a blinding flash as Mac's photographer ignited his powder tray for the photograph.

For a split second, Thad looked dazed, then, turning, he lifted a hand and pointed a long, wrathful finger at Mac and shouted, "Fornicater!"

"You're wrong there, preacher!" a man shouted from the audience, and the hushed shock exploded into laughter.

Mac bounded off the stool, his erect shaft still exposed, and shouted, "Kill him! Shoot all of them!"

Slocum moved quickly, putting himself between Thad and the six thugs making their way up the aisle toward the stage. "Don't do it," he shouted, leveling the shotgun.

The audience crowded the aisles, flowing away from the six men.

"You! You bastard!" Mac yelled, now recognizing Slocum in spite of the makeup. And with that, he rushed the big Southerner.

Slocum brought the butt end up quick, hitting Mac hard in the chest and knocking the man back off his feet. "You men, drop your guns," Slocum ordered the thugs. "He ain't worth dying for."

The hired guns, sensing something had changed in Mac's standing in the community, slowly drew their side arms and dropped them to the floor.

The crowd had stopped moving now, frozen in curiosity at the back of the theater.

"And you folks," Slocum yelled, still holding the shotgun, "you all should be ashamed. Ashamed from letting *that* cheat you and lie to you."

"You heard me, kill him," Mac bellowed, trying to regain his feet. "I still run things around here. Kill him!"

None of Mac's hired guns answered. They stood there, frozen, as if the spectacle in front of them rendered them unable to move.

"I say this, you people go home and think about what kind of town you want," Slocum shouted to the crowd gathered at the back of the theater. "Go home and figure a way to pay Mac what you owe him. Find an honest bank that will loan it to you, then pay him."

The crowd let out a small murmur.

Then a voice behind Slocum said, "I say you drop that scattergun."

Slocum turned to the left of the stage and saw one of Mac's hired guns holding a pistol to the back of Joseph's head. He hesitated, looking from the audience, who could not see Joseph and the gunman. The young actor's face was wet with sweat and his eyes widened with genuine fear.

Slocum loosened his grip on the gun, then set it gently down on the edge of the stage.

Mac, now sizing up the situation, saw that perhaps someone had dealt him a set of new cards. He scampered to his feet and raced to the podium. "Friends, friends, friends," he shouted. "You all know me. I live among you. I work among you. We have all sweated and toiled to build this city together."

"But you own her," a voice from the back called. "You own every stick and pebble."

"The hell with a bank," someone else called. "If we killed you, what would happen?"

It was turning bad. Slocum could feel it. The crowd at the back of the theater was turning into a lynch mob. Some of them had labored for Mac for years without seeing a dime in their pocket. Now they were more than willing to take revenge.

"Listen to me, my friends," Mac said, showing the murmuring crowd his upraised palms. "This is our town. Paradise is ours, every man, woman, and child."

"It will be," someone called and a few of the men, miners, broke from the crowd toward the stage.

Mac's face changed again as fear swelled up into his eyes, contorting his mouth. "Stop! Stop it, damn you!" he shouted, then ran to the edge of the stage and dragged Joseph out by his shirtfront, the gunman, still holding a pistol up behind the actor's ear, following.

The men heading for the stage stopped at the sight.

"One more step, you ignorant sonsofbitches, and the boy dies!" Mac shouted.

A low gasp rose from the back of the theater.

"Listen to me now, you ignorant rabble," Mac shouted. "There is not a man here who does not owe me. That's the truth, like it or not. There's not a man among you ignorant scum who doesn't work for me."

"We work for you, that don't mean you own us," a brave soul at the back shouted.

"That's exactly what it means!" Mac shouted back. "The people I work for and I own you. Every one of you. What do you think happens if you kill me? They'll hang whoever did it. And then they'll just send someone else.

And you'll work for him. There's not a man here that hasn't signed his name or put his mark on a piece of paper that says I own you.''

The crowd seemed to deflate, its murmuring growing weak, dying away.

''Now, listen to me,'' Mac said. ''You leave now, all of you. You all go back to work. Go back to your homes. And I'll forget this. Tomorrow it will be like it never happened.''

''But it did happen, Mac,'' Kate's voice boomed from backstage.

Slocum turned toward the voice and saw her walk out now, holding a shotgun.

''Thought I'd join this little performance,'' she said, holding the shotgun on Mac's hired gun. ''Now, it's my turn to talk. Why don't you tell them how you bought half the state government? Or how your books don't keep the right track on what folks have paid in. Tell 'em that, Mac.''

''I'll kill this boy,'' Mac's gunman whispered to Kate. ''One more move, I'll kill him.''

''Kill him, he's nothing to me,'' Kate said. ''But you kill him, and you'll be dead before he hits the ground. You want to die for that fat bastard's money?''

''Not today,'' the gunmen said and pulled the pistol away from Joseph's head.

''Now, you pick up that shotgun,'' Kate ordered Slocum.

Slocum did as she said. ''I figure we should take him to jail,'' he said. ''Probably be safe there.''

And with that, Kate and Slocum marched Mac off the stage.

•   •   •

For two nights, the crowd stayed outside the jail, yelling taunts at Mac. And for two days, Kate stayed holed up in Mac's office, going over the ledgers. If running a whorehouse had taught her nothing else, it was how to figure numbers.

At the end of the second full day, Kate came into the jail and sat down on the chair by the sheriff's desk. Slocum, behind the desk, was eating a plate of eggs. "You find anything?" he asked.

"I was right," she said. "He was sending money back, but he was stealing, too. By my figures, half, maybe more of the people he has down for loans paid them off a long time ago. He cleared the accounts with his bosses, but kept the people working."

"What about the other half?"

"I can't tell for sure, but it looks like they worked for him," Kate said. "He went into business for himself, buying up land last year from those that owned it. He was out to cheat the ones he worked for back East. Can't say I have much sympathy for them."

"Five thousand dollars, Slocum!" Mac yelled from his cell in the back. "You hear me? Five thousand."

Kate turned to where Mac yelled. "He been doing that right along?" she asked.

"Keeps getting bigger," Slocum said, forking a helping of eggs into his mouth. "Started out yesterday at two thousand. He ups the price every couple of hours."

20

"Don't you ever, ever interrupt my lines again," Thad said.

It was two days later and Thad, Viv, Joseph, and Slocum were sitting in the small dining room of the hotel. The actors were planning on leaving the next day and the clerk had the saloon fix up four fancy steak dinners. Now, well fed, the four sat back in their chairs, talking quietly.

"Frankly, I didn't see much of a choice," Slocum answered, smiling.

"Neither did I," Viv answered. "I would have kissed him, like we planned, but he had other ideas."

"Has anybody seen him?" Slocum asked. Mac had eluded the man charged with bringing him over to the barber for a bath and a shave on the fourth day. Whether he had somehow brought his freedom from the man or genuinely escaped was never made clear. Without a horse or supplies, whichever way he ran wasn't going to be pleasant for him. Oddly, the man's negligence or corruption hadn't even earned him a beating. Mostly, people just didn't care if Mac vanished.

"The boys down at the saloon say he took off after that photographer," Joseph answered. "The photographer high-tailed it back to San Francisco with the plate. He figured on showing it to Mac's bosses there, then sending it back East. Figured maybe he could get some kind of reward."

Slocum had to smile at that. Somehwere back East in a fancy office, a group of men would open a package holding the picture of Mac. He wondered what they would think.

"I haven't seen Kate, either," Viv said. "She took out of here like someone was chasing her."

"She's gone to Carson City," Slocum said. "Me and her started looking over the papers, contracts in Mac's office, and most of them, they didn't look legal. She went to find a lawyer who really knows how to read them."

"Dear lad, I hope you realize what we've done," Thad said, staring across the table at Slocum.

"I know we chased a thievin' bastard out of town," Slocum answered.

"We've chased not just a thievin' bastard, as you so eloquently say, out of town, but the town's mayor, law, banker, businessman, and who knows what else," Thad said. "It's doubtful Paradise will survive a year."

"It'll survive," Slocum said. "It's a good town, the people are good people. They'll figure it out."

"I take it, then, you have no qualms about the 'good people' acquiring the property owned by Mac's employers?" Thad asked.

Slocum thought on this for a moment, then said, "There was a town here before Mac moved in. Just because he built a few buildings doesn't mean he owned the town or the people. If those contracts are no good, then those that the syndicate owe money to, they can buy those buildings and the mines."

"Still, he did make a town," Thad said.

"He made it, but he wasn't going to keep it, even if we did nothing," Slocum answered.

Thad leaned back and contemplated this. "You sound pretty sure of yourself, lad."

"My experience, I learned that folks will work for a bastard if they're paid enough," Slocum said. "They may not like it, but they'll do it for themselves. Probably they won't do a good job of it, either. And they'll work for a leader, a genuine leader, if they don't see that much in their own pockets. They'll do it because they think what they're doing is worthwhile. But folks will never work for a bastard without seeing something in their own pockets or building something for themselves. Maybe Mac could have held this town for a little while longer, but not much."

"Well, it's been a genuine pleasure, Mr. Slocum," Viv said." "But right now I believe I need my sleep."

"I, too, sir, must retire," Thad announced. "We have a long trip tomorrow and not much time to accomplish those miles."

Epilogue

Slocum left early in the morning, as the sun was just beginning to turn the sky the shade of blue he liked. It was a ride to Carson City, but if the truth were told, he was now hungry to be on his own. He longed for the calm of a lonely trail and the time to think over what had happened in Paradise.

No one, save the stable boy, saw him leave. He rode down the empty street at a slow walk, wondering what Paradise would look like in a year or in ten years.

As he passed Kate's house, he saw a flash of material, gingham in the bushes, maybe ten yards back. It was one of Kate's girls, the one who was forever standing by the road waiting for something to pass.

Slocum waved and saw the girl come forward.

"Kate ain't here," she said, stepping into the road.

"I know," Slocum said.

"You leaving now?" she asked, bringing her hands together in front of her to clasp them.

"That's what I was doing."

"Then you take care of yourself," the girl said. "And you come back sometime."

"I'll try," Slocum answered, and heeled the spotted horse forward.

When he was well away from Kate's, he turned the horse onto an old trail and followed it up into the hills. As the sun was just starting its slant to the western horizon, he turned onto a trail he was pretty certain would take him north to Carson City.

He figured on making camp around dusk.

The fire had just started to go good and Slocum began to feed it larger lengths of wood. The clearing, where he had made camp, was just about as pretty a spot as he had seen in a long time. It smelled of sweet pine and the brook a few yards away had yielded a half dozen fat trout.

Slocum found it hard to believe that Paradise and that mess was only a day's ride behind him. Now, in the early evening, alone up in the hills, he could feel himself relax for the first time in a long time.

Kate, of course, was gone. The lawyer in Carson City had, in fact, found most of Mac's contracts to be unlawful and she sent word back that she would need to stay in order to work out the legal matters with the state's attorney. It would, she said, take the better part of a year.

Slocum took one of the gutted fish from the pile near the fire, skewered it with a slim stick, then leaned it toward the fire. The fish burned and crackled, releasing its fresh scent.

The sun's last rays were slanting through the trees and night's first shadows were collecting around the small camp when Slocum heard the snap of a branch.

Holding his breath, he waited, letting his gun hand slip down toward his holster.

Another twig snapped and Slocum stood, his eyes searching the darkening trees in the direction of the sound.

Then he saw him. A man approached from the far end of the clearing. Thin and gaunt, he walked slowly, leading a swaybacked horse by the halter.

As he came into the clearing, the man raised a hand and smiled. "I saw your fire from the trail," the stranger said, still smiling, "and thought I'd come visiting."

Seeing that the stranger was unarmed, Slocum relaxed his gun hand. The man wore all black, from his cracked and worn boots to the battered, wide-brimmed hat on his head. "Got some fish here, you're welcome to a share," Slocum said, motioning toward his catch.

"Praise the lord," the stranger said, his smile widening.

"You a preacher?" Slocum asked.

"That I am, sir," the man answered, extending a hand toward Slocum.

Slocum took the hand and shook it firmly. The man had more muscle in him than Slocum would have thought. "What kind of preacher are you?" he asked, knowing his question would seem strange to the man.

"Fair to middling, I'd like to think," the preacher answered earnestly. "Been ministering to the ranchers and miners up north lately. One man, a family, ten men, it doesn't matter, the Lord hears all prayers."

"I'd like to think so," Slocum said.

"Heard about a town near here. Paradise, is it?" the preacher asked.

"I just come from there," Slocum said. "About a two-day ride."

"And when you were there, did you see a need for a preacher?" came the next question. "I mean in your own opinion, that is?"

Now Slocum had to smile. "They need one, and they even have a place for you to preach in. Brand-new theater, as fine as you'd ever like to see."

"Praise," the preacher said, excitedly. "Please, tell me more."

"Go hitch your horse next to mine, then I'll tell you while we eat some of this fish," Slocum answered. "It's a long story and I'm going to need a little time to tell it right."

J. L. REASONER

AUTHOR OF *RIVERS OF GOLD*

___*Healer's Calling*___   0-425-15487-4/$5.99

On the bloody battlefields of the Civil War,
Sara Black had proven her courage and skill
as a medic. Now, the war had ended, but she
had found her true calling: to become one of
America's first woman doctors.
(June '96)

___*The Healer's Road*___   0-515-11762-5/$5.99

When his parents died because of a lack of
proper medicine, Thomas Black vowed to
become a doctor and better people's lives.
Now, with the advent of war, he is challenged
to provide better care than ever before–in a
fraction of the time. During the savage conflict
of the Civil War, Thomas Black, and his two
children who follow in his footsteps, will embody
the true nobility of the American spirit.